MUTINY

ALSO BY BENJAMIN VOGT

Revolt

Book 1 in the Revolt Trilogy

MUTINY

BENJAMIN VOGT

To my superhero of an editor, Stacey. Without you, none of this would be possible.

"But my dreams, they aren't as empty as my conscious seems to be."

PETE TOWNSHEND

CHAPTER ONE

I t takes me weeks to decently walk. I spend hours at a time limping around my frigid cell, unrelenting until I can take ten steps without holding onto the wall for support.

My fingers drift along the scratch marks etched into the cold cement.

That crash messed me up. It's a blessing that I'm stuck in my cell until the warden says otherwise. It gives me more than enough time to heal. More importantly, it gives me enough time to plan a way out of this hell hole and start my subsequent course of action-killing Matthew White.

A jolt of pain surges up my thigh like a blast of electricity, causing me to stop in the middle of my cell. I swear, limping over to my unforgivingly firm mattress.

That's enough walking for right now.

I gingerly place myself on the mattress, rest my back up against the cold thick cement wall, and breathe, letting the jolt in my thigh simmer down to a dull throb.

I'm absolutely sick of pain and its relentless companionship.

A little bang against my cell door disrupts my languishing. A

Saint peers through the tiny rectangular window placed toward the top of the grey-ish metal.

"Here's the leftover slop," he says with a snide grin on his face. "Get it while it's cold."

I don't respond.

"Don't make me repeat myself."

"I'm not hungry."

"Well that's too bad, now ain't it? Get up and get over here, now."

I sluggishly rise from my mattress.

"Here," he says, opening the door's metal slide. "Bon appétit."

He carelessly hands me the tray, spilling a bit of the slop in the process. He then shuts the slide, turning away before screaming, *"Light's out!"*

Circular blots flash in my vision as my eyes try to soak in the abrupt blackness. I'm still not used to this. Like clockwork, a monotone voice spills out from Salem's p.a. system, listing off our nightly procedures.

"Attention inmates. It is now light's out. Any prisoner caught out between now and when the alarm sounds off in the morning will be shot. Any loud noises will be investigated. The alarm will commence in three. . . two. . . one. . ."

I flinch at the ear-piercing wail of the prison siren. It lasts for thirty seconds, and then an eerie silence replaces the din. I sharply inhale and then exhale with unease. I lose all sense of direction during light's out, not to mention the sheer horror of not being able to see. My eyes don't adjust, so I find myself stumbling around a lot more while finding my way back to my bed.

Sitting down, I force in a mouthful of slop. The cuisine shares the same texture as a moldy sponge; chunks stick to the roof of my mouth, and I dry retch. My stomach churns, and my eyes water. I need the calories, so I force it in before tossing the tray to the floor, allowing a metallic thud to echo out.

I lie down across the top of the mattress, pulling the thin sheet up to my chin, keenly aware of my numb toes. They're turning purple.

I shiver and try to imagine the sun beating down on me. We don't get shoes, and a guy froze to death recently. I'm sure they keep it cold to keep us all in line. It's kinda hard to get into trouble when your entire body is unresponsive.

It won't stop me, though.

I have a plan to find Raphael and Chloe the second I'm let out of my cell. I hope they're still breathing after all the torture they were put through. They're my only hope of busting out of here. I can't do it alone.

I lie my head on my pillow, attempting to ignore my chattering teeth and shivering body.

Salem is a forsaken hell hole.

I turn over, cupping my hands around my mouth and breathe hard into them. It doesn't really help. I breathe harder, but nothing comes of it. I would do anything for a steaming hot shower right about now.

My heart lurches as the sound of my door being unlocked echoes throughout the room. My eyes search the darkness for the disturbance. A chill slides down my spine as the creaky door begins to skid open.

"This is him, right?" an unknown voice asks.

"Yep," another voice responds. Before I can think, someone's got a hold of both my feet.

I'm dragged from the bed, landing on the stiff cement floor.

"Get offa me!" I blurt.

I get slapped across the face, "*Shhh!* Make another noise and I'll carve your eyes out."

I clamp my teeth. My legs strain in agony as I'm dragged out of my cell. I can't see anything, but one thing is for sure; these aren't Saints. My kidnapper's grip is tight, but not as strong as a soldier's; a Saint's hands are heavy and firm, not scrawny and brittle.

I'm dragged for what feels like minutes, stopping when my feet are dropped to the floor. I try to scramble upright but get kicked back down to the ground.

My chest heaves up and down, and my fingers curl up into fists.

"Get a light on him," somebody demands. My eyes slam shut as the area comes to life with illumination.

Seconds pass before I'm able to open them again, seeing flashlight beams pointed down at my face. I cover my eyes with my hand, squinting.

The light is moved away, and a few feet to my left, I hear someone struggling.

"Who are you guys?" I ask, blinking away the blobs of color from my vision.

"Wouldn't you like to know?" one asks, and I see that his jumpsuit is sprinkled in blood.

I blink some more, "Take me back to my cell."

Another man laughs, "You think you get to make demands?" he pauses. "Bring him to his feet."

The two kidnappers aggressively lift me upright. My shins ache as my heels touch the floor.

More commotion fills the room, so I turn my head, seeing an inmate with his head being forced into a pool of water filled up in one of the sinks. He gargles, struggling to escape but fails.

"What do you want from me?" I ask, my eyes narrowed.

"Silas Delgado sends his regards," another mutters, ignoring me.

One of the assailants grab my shoulders and shoves me toward a sink near the other drowning convict. I struggle, but the crash left me too vulnerable. I attempt to get a good breath, but it's cut short when my face is shoved into the pool of water.

My heart speeds up.

"Make sure the freak dies," the muffled voice barks an order. "Don't let the boss down."

My lungs begin to burn.

Who are these people? How did they get out of their cells?

My mind fogs, my lungs burn, and I'm about to pass out when the back of my head is released; like a stretched rubber band being unconstrained, my face flies out of the water, but I get punched in the jaw before I can gasp. I stumble backward and fall to the floor. My attacker throws another punch, but a blade penetrates the side of his throat and stops him permanently.

Blood gushes out onto the cold, wet tile.

I sputter for air, "R-Raph?"

A smirk splashes and he parts his lips to reply, but a fist gets hurled into the side of his head, and he crashes into one of the sinks. His attacker throws another punch, but Raphael is faster; he thrusts his knife into the man's eye socket.

The assailant screams, grasping his wound with both hands before tripping over his buddy's corpse and smacking his head against the floor with a sickening crack. Raphael finishes him off, and then goes after the next inmate in the room.

I scooch back against a bathroom stall, watching my partner take out the rest of the prisoners-brutal and unmerciful. They try to fight back, but none of them stand a chance against him.

"Nice to see you," I remark, observing the room littered with corpses.

"Ditto," he strides over to me, reaching his hand out for mine to grab. "Can you walk?"

"Yeah, but it would suck."

He purses his lips together and replies, "What if I help balance you?"

I shrug, "We can try."

He helps me to my feet, propping his arm under my armpit to steady me. We hobble out of the showers and turn right.

"Who were those guys?" I ask, while the familiar, sharp pain surges through both legs.

"There's this idiot in here named Silas. He's the leader of this gang, and he doesn't know when to back off."

"What did he want with me?"

"Well, we had some disagreements. He wanted to recruit you, and I told him that if he touched you, then he'd be gagging on his own tongue."

"And then?"

"I killed one of his guys, and I guess to get back at me he wanted to off you. Some kid told me his plans, so that's how I knew when to come and save your unfortunate hide."

"That kid he's referring to is me," a stalker says from behind.

Raphael and I turn around. We can't see him due to the lack of light.

"The name's Blaine, but most people around here call me Exodus."

"Exodus?" I ask, feeling an eyebrow rise with the question.

"Yep. . . now get out of here. Make sure to tell him our plan."

"I will. We'll see you in the morning," Raphael answers the darkness.

"Alright, see ya," the unseen footfalls make their way down the hall.

Raphael leads me back down the corridor.

"That's the guy that helped you find me?" I ask, a sudden sharp twinge of pain jolts up my legs.

"Yeah. He knows about everything there is to know about Salem."

"What's the plan he was talking about?"

"Just wait until I get you back to your cell, then I'll tell you."

"Fair enough."

We take a left at the end of the hall, then a right down the next, and eventually we make it back to my partially opened cell. The guards didn't notice that I've been gone, so I quietly slip inside.

Raphael gets ready to lock me in, "You ready for me to tell you?"

"Of course."

He waits a moment, "We know a way out of here."

My eyes widen, "Seriously?"

"Seriously. Exodus is the one with the plan. I didn't believe him, but he showed me – it'll just take some luck; and luck, my friend, is always on my side," he pauses. "We're gonna make it out of here *alive*, Pinder. We're going to finish what we started."

He shuts the door, leaving me with my exhilarated thoughts.

CHAPTER TWO

G loom seeps from the sky, dripping smog into the air, and the overwhelming smell of gunpowder and blood fill my nostrils. Simon is forced to his knees, and I watch as Matthew carves a smile into his throat. My best friend collapses, face-first, into the dirt, gurgling on his own gore. His fingers twitch.

※

MY EYES FLASH OPEN, AND MY BREATHING CONSTRICTS. All the lights in my cell are on, and the electronic hum of my door being unlocked bounces through my ears. I sit up shockingly and painfully fast. The adrenaline fuels my muscles but fails to deaden the relentless and unforgiving pain.

It's silent, but a moment later my door flies open and two Saints grab me out of my bed and force me to stand. I form a protest but get shoved out of the room and down a hallway before I can form any words with my cracked lips.

"Warden Yale isn't too pleased with you," one of them states.

I grit my teeth, pain shooting up my shins, "I'm not supposed to be let out of my cell."

The other Saint glances at me, his ski mask obscuring most of his features, "He thought that too. Guess you took a little trip last night, Prisoner 31103."

My stomach churns, and I feel the sudden urge to vomit despite barely having enough food in my stomach as it is.

They escort me up three sets of stairs and down two different corridors before we stop in front of a door with a mess of words stenciled into the metal. My dyslexia is fully functional, and I can't read it, but I already know it's the warden's office.

His cramped office is occupied by a wooden desk that lies dead in the center; the Warden hunches in the chair behind it. Raphael and some kid with bleached skin, bleached hair, and pale blue eyes wait in two plain chairs in front of the desk. There's one empty seat next to them that's meant for me.

"Come take a seat, will you?" Warden Yale mumbles, a scowl glued to his wrinkle-riddled face. His nose is perched in the center of face and looks sharper than a blade.

I don't comply. My two escorts shove me into the chair, causing my teeth to grind painfully against each other.

"So," Warden Yale's raspy, antiquated voice starts the conversation. "How was your evening last night, Mr. Pinder?"

I don't speak.

"I see that you're still a man of few words," he glares.

"Only around you," Raphael chimes in.

Warden Yale snaps his fingers. One of the Saints grabs the back of Raphael's head and crashes his face down onto the desk, holding it there.

"Get your hands off of me! Do you have any idea who I am?" he blurts.

Yale ignores his outburst, turning his gaze to me, "My security director came to me this fine morning and showed me some footage from last night. I saw you, Mr. Ramirez, and Mr. West in one of Salem's corridors having a casual conversation as if on a break. Would you mind telling me why you three were outside your cells, and how you got there?"

Raphael snarls, "You pathetic waste of space. You know you can't touch me *or* Jason. We're off limits."

The warden leans back in his chair, a wicked grin appearing across his face, "Right you are, sir. However, Mr. West isn't." He snaps his fingers once more. "Let's show these two what happens when they disobey Salem and her rules."

One of the soldiers grabs the bleached kid and hurls him on top of the desk, causing paperwork and books to flee from their resting places and scatter all around the office. The other one grabs a flashlight from his belt, walks over to the prisoner, and shines the bright light into his eyes.

He screams while thrashing around. The first soldier holds him down, and the second forcefully pries the inmate's eyelids apart, using his other hand to illuminate his iris.

I raise an eyebrow. *Why would a light to his eyes be causing this much pain?*

The soldiers take turns slamming their fists into the inmate's gut. Then, one of them picks a heavy book from up off the floor and bashes it into the kid's face, forcing specks of blood to fly out of his mouth and nose.

Raphael and I are forced to watch. We twist in our chairs and an occasional twitch makes its way to our eyes. After a few minutes, they throw the kid to the ground, giving him a few more kicks to end the torture.

"Get these three down to the cafeteria," Warden Yale orders. His gaze settles on Raphael and me, "If you two pull any more stunts, I'll have your friend chopped up into little tiny pieces, understand? And don't think this is the end; I'll find out how you got out of your cells."

The two soldiers force us to our feet and escort the three of us to the cafeteria. When they turn around and leave, Raphael introduces me to the bleached kid with a bloody nose and a busted lip as Exodus.

That wasn't too hard to guess.

He's pissed off and won't stop covering his eyes with his palms.

"Why'd they shine a light into your eyes?" I ask, uncomfortable at the number of inmates that are staring at us as we stride through the mess hall and over to the food trays.

"My eyes are sensitive to light," he answers with blood shining across his gritted teeth. "It's a medical condition. I guess you could say I have Albinism, hence the white hair and skin, but I'm pretty sure you were smart enough to guess that, huh?"

"That sucks. You're young, what are you doing in here?"

"Heh, young? I could ask you the same thing. My dad was serving a triple life sentence; he died the first week, and I inherited his sentence. I've been in here since I was fourteen."

My eyes widen at this, "Wait, seriously? How old are you now?"

"Nineteen, you?"

"Well, that depends. What month is it?"

"October."

"Then I'm eighteen."

I missed my own birthday, Chloe's too.

The thought of her makes me yearn to escape, her at my side, the two of us together.

Raphael grabs a tray, "Enough with the small talk. Tell him how we're going to get out of here, Blaine."

Exodus nods, "I will, just wait until we can get a seat, and the pain in my friggin' eyes go away."

After we're given our slop and a portion of water, the three of us make it over to an inmate-free table. After taking a few bites, Exodus gives me the details.

"Every Thursday, a cargo boat docks on the island."

"The island?" I interrupt. "What island?"

Raphael chimes in, "You know about Alcatraz, Pinder?"

"Sorta, yeah."

"The prison was torn down years back and replaced by Salem."

I ponder the implications of this newly discovered fact, "We're in San Francisco? How are we supposed to make it back to land if we're on an island?"

Exodus sighs, "Well maybe if you'd let me talk and finish, you could find out."

"Sorry. Go on."

"Like I was saying, every Thursday night a cargo boat docks on the island to deliver food and water to the inmates. Well, at the same time, all the Saints –minus the ones who're patrolling– are sent up to the fifth floor to have their weekly meeting with the Warden," he pauses, taking another bite out of his food. "There's a hatch that leads up to the roof. We get up there undetected, climb down Salem—."

"*Climb* down?" I ask, flinching at the thought of scaling the sides of the infamous prison. I can't help but tremble at the pain I imagine myself going through. I'm not healing fast enough.

"Yes, *climb* down. Then we hijack that boat, and *Voilà*, we're out."

I stare at him in awe, "How did you figure all of this out?"

He keeps his eyes closed, "When you've been in this cesspit for five years, you learn the gist of things."

"How come you haven't escaped yet, then?"

"No motivation. I'd have nowhere to go, nothing to do, so what would be the point?"

"What changed your mind?"

He smirks, "I got bored."

Raphael grins, "Tell Jason how we're going to get out of our cells after lights out."

"I'm sure you were told who Silas Delgado is, right?"

I nod my head, "Considering that he tried to have his men drown me in a sink, I'm well aware of him and his pissy little gang."

"Awhile back he bribed one of the Saints and got a keycard. His keycard will unlock any cell, or door in this entire place. We get it, and we're golden."

I turn to Raphael, "How did you two get out of your cell last night without the card?"

He takes a sip of his water, "Simple really. We smuggled two trays out of this here fine eatery and used them to keep the doors from shutting; but it isn't foolproof, which is why we're stealing the keycard."

Exodus nods, "Exactly."

I force in a disgusting spoonful of slop, and after unsticking it from the roof of my mouth with my tongue, swallow, "I'm impressed."

Raphael's grin hasn't left, "This is legit going to happen. We're going to make it out of this place."

"But before we leave," I say. "We have to get Chloe. Do you know where she is?"

"Yeah, in the female ward, but it won't be easy."

"Who cares? Once we get that keycard, we'll break her out and leave."

Exodus finishes off his slop, "Cool beans. Today is Wednesday, so this goes down tomorrow night."

Raphael and I agree. I decide to keep my slowly healing injuries a quiet grievance.

One of the two Saints who are watching over the cafeteria speak up, "Attention all prisoners, it is now time for your daily chores. Line up."

I take one last bite from my slop before standing up. Raphael and Exodus do the same. Every inmate in the cafeteria heads to a wall and lines up in some kind of order.

The two Saints begin marching down the streak of convicts, assigning each individual a different job: laundry, kitchen, or toilets. Exodus is given laundry, Raphael's given kitchen, and unfortunately, I'm tasked with toilets.

CHAPTER THREE

S crubbing crap-stained porcelain isn't how I wanted to spend the first day out of my cell. It's almost like some of these animals screw up their own toilets on *purpose*, leaving it to those unlucky prisoners assigned to clean up after them.

The two Saints who are supposed to be supervising us walked off, so the sixteen other inmates who are joining me in this disgusting adventure are mostly messing around. We're cleaning cellblock one, and there's one of us in each cell.

I stand to take a look at my work. The toilet's scrubbed to my satisfaction. I turn around and walk out of the cell, and three other prisoners from the cell ahead of me raise their voices.

"You think you're all special, don't you, prick?"

My eyes snap to them, my adrenaline spikes, but they aren't talking to me. Two of them are backing a third tall and scrawny inmate against the wall near the yet-to-be-cleaned john.

"I never said that," the victim mutters, his voice surprisingly deep. "Now back off before I tell our escorts about your freaks' little gift exchange last Friday. The second they shake you down and find those shanks, it won't be all too pretty, now will it?"

The two inmates exchange looks, their expressions turning sinister.

"Oh, so you're gonna snitch, huh Bruno? Is that what you're going to do?" one asks.

His buddy snarls, "Yeah, you gonna drop a dime on us, Bruno?"

Bruno raises his hands to calm them down, "Now listen, I shouldn't have said tha—"

The two prisoners shove him to the floor, each taking turns kicking him in the face until blood pools out of his mouth. They then grab him by the scruff of the neck and slam his nose against the toilet.

"*Stop! Somebody help! Please!*" he cries.

His face is slammed back down against the porcelain, tinging the water inside rosy red.

My feet motion forward, but I stop them. I have second thoughts clouding my mind. If I intervene, it could compromise tomorrow's escape. I choose to stay still, watching as the two inmates drown Bruno in the bloody toilet water and toss his lifeless body to the ground. When they notice their audience they place their index fingers up to their lips, both shaking their heads violently.

"Hey, guards!" one of them shouts, using a false sense of urgency. "This guy just tried to attack us."

It takes only a few moments before our two escorts come rushing into the cell. They take turns examining the dead body. The two prisoners insist that Bruno started it, but the Saints don't care. Instead they walk away, telling all of us not to waste their time.

⚔

"BASHED HIS FACE IN, HUH?" EXODUS ASKS AS THE TWO of us approach the serving line.

"Yeah, man, it was insane." I grab a tray, and my shins burn as I make my way over to Raphael, who's standing behind the serving line dishing the inmates up.

"How was scrubbing?" he asks when I stop in front of him.

I shake my head, "Terrible. My hands still smell like crap."

He laughs, "You think that's bad? You don't even wanna know how we make this food, Pinder."

"You aren't wrong."

"Never am. Here."

He slaps down a few scoops of slop onto my tray before handing me a small cup of water. I thank him before moving on, heading toward a table near the back of the room and saving a place for Exodus.

After getting served, he makes his way over to me. He sits down and instantly starts eating.

"So, how was laundry?" I ask.

He swallows, "Disgusting as usual."

I take a sip of water, "I wonder if the female ward is better?"

"Doubt it. Females are. . . interesting."

I chuckle.

"Okay, so I need your help," he says, taking in another mouthful of slop.

"With what?"

He swallows, "I need you to get the crap beat outta you."

"What?"

"Like I said this morning, Silas has a keycard. It's back in his cell, and I plan on stealing it."

"What does that have to do with me getting beaten?"

"Well, if he finds out it's missing, it'll be bad. So, I need you to frame him."

"Frame him?"

"Well, yeah. Yale doesn't want anyone to touch you, so if you can get Silas and his boys to knock you into next week, he'll have them taken away to get tortured, or better yet, killed."

I take a slow bite out of my slop, "My body is still broken, man. I don't know if Raphael told you, but we got into a major car crash."

"Oh yeah, I know. When I first met Raphael, he wasn't in the best shape. Look, you have all the time in the world to heal up after we get out of here. Let that be your motivation."

I stare at him, unamused, "What if they kill me, man?"

"They won't. The Saints will break it up."

I let out a resigned sigh, "What table is he at?"

Exodus gestures with his head at a table near the serving line, "See the man with the shaved head and face tats? That's him. Just go up and get a rise out of him. Once the Saints leave their post to help you, I'll sneak out of the cafeteria and find his cell. Remember, play the victim when you're rescued. Frame Silas, and make sure he's taken away."

I reluctantly nod, "I got it, and you're *sure* this idiot has a keycard?"

"Yeah, how else did his men kidnap you last night? Trust me, dude."

I stand from our table, taking a deep breath, "Alright, I'll trust you."

"Dope."

Staring over at the man surrounded by gangsters, I prepare myself mentally and physically for some of the most excruciating pain I'm ever going to face in my life.

CHAPTER FOUR

A t the head of Silas' table, I cross swords with the biggest
gangster in Salem, "So, you're the *miserable* piss-face that
had his men kidnap me last night and attempt to drown me in a
sink, huh?"

He shoots daggers at me, "Get away from my table before I
bash your brains in, freak."

I chuckle, hoping my stomach's churning doesn't give me
away, "How sad is it that a handful of your boys couldn't take me
down?"

He abruptly stands, "You've got quite the mouth on you, kid,"
he cracks his knuckles. "Warden says he doesn't want anyone to
touch a hair on your precious little head, but the offer is really
tempting."

"Why don't you take it, then?" I ask, raising my arms at my
side in submission. "If it'll calm your tiny little girl nerves, then
take your best shot. C'mon, Silas, punch me."

He growls. My stomach growls louder in protest as he steps
out from his table and stomps toward me.

"Maybe I will," he breathes, his eyes narrow.

I spit on his face, and stars explode in my vision as his fist connects with my cheek. I stumble back a few steps, and another fist crashes into my face.

My chest ignites with a fire. It isn't fear. It's rage, and even though my legs threaten to shatter, I charge at Silas, throwing him against the table and bashing my fists into his nose. Fury stokes the blaze and fuels my blows until his blood stains my knuckles.

One of his gangsters bashes a tray into my shoulder, causing me to let go of Silas.

"You're dead!" my new attacker shouts. He swings again, but I catch the tray midair, prying it out of his hands and planting its metal edge into the side of his skull.

He drops to the floor, and Silas grabs me from behind. Another gangster approaches the battle. He hammers his fists into my gut, and I kick his kneecap which sends him buckling to the floor screaming.

I blurt out a swear; the kick I just sent out sends a shock of pain up my leg.

Silas wraps his hands around my face, attempting to twist my neck, but I stomp down on his bare foot. He releases me instantly. I keep adding to the agony surging through my lower body.

Stop using your feet.

Another assailant approaches me. I anticipate his oncoming punch, but someone shoves me from behind and I crash into the floor. In a daze, I try to keep up with the ongoing flurry of kicks and punches thrown at me; my entire face goes numb, warm liquid spills from my mouth and nose, and the corners of my vision grow dark.

As I welcome the numbness that comes with a restful blackout, the harsh voice of a Saint orders the prisoners to stand down, keeping the blackout from enfolding me in its arms. The prisoners don't listen. It takes a bullet to the back of one of their heads to gain their attention. The gangster collapses, his skull exposed. The rest of the inmates back off.

The sudden light from the cafeteria sends my brain into a frenzy. My entire head begins to ache.

"This prisoner is off limits!" one soldier blurts.

I look up at him, blood streaming out of my nose like a river, "I didn't do anything wrong. That *prick* just came up and started throwing swings."

The two Saints stare at Silas. Without another second passing, they each take a hold of him and haul him off like a toddler who's about to get disciplined by a harsh, abusive father.

"What're you doing!" he blurts, spit flying from the corners of his lips.

"Anyone who touches Prisoner 31103 has to deal with Warden Yale. Now shut up before I send two bullets through your head."

Silas' eyes widen, baring his yellow teeth, "You're dead, kid! You hear me?"

A soldier pistol whips the back of his head. His shark-like, black eyes roll up, and his body goes limp.

I gradually sit up, blood dripping onto the floor from my nose. When I get a sense of which way is up, I get to my feet, instantly wanting to fall back over. The pain is so sharp and fresh. It hurts *so* bad.

I spit a bit of blood from my mouth, staining the floor some more. I then limp back to my table, sitting down before my legs give out.

This escape plan better work.

A few more Saints enter the room and drag the deceased inmates out of the cafeteria; the one that was shot, and the other that has the tray bashed into his head. Raphael approaches my table and takes a seat next to me.

"I saw Exodus sneak out," he says, taking a bite out of his slop. "I'm guessing you getting beat up was a part of his overall plan?"

I nod, "I had to frame Silas so Exodus could go and steal the keycard out of his cell."

"Good idea. You alright?"

"Does it look like it?"

"Not really, but I know what will make you feel better."

"What?"

"I'm sneaking over to the female ward tonight to tell Frye our plan."

"Did you ever figure out how we're going to break her out of there tomorrow?"

He shakes his head, "No, haven't given it much thought, but I will. I promise that this will all go down without a hitch."

"Okay, good."

Exodus pops up behind us a few minutes later, "Sup fellas? Geez, man, you're a mess."

I shake my head, "Hmmm, I wonder why?"

He ignores me, "Okay, so I got the keycard and hid it in my cell. What happened to Silas? Give me all of the juicy details, dude."

"He got taken away," I reply. "Warden Yale is probably torturing him as we speak."

"Good."

"I'm going to need the keycard tonight," Raphael says. "I'm going to go tell Chloe our plan. On the way back, I'll delete all the footage. That way, Warden won't chop you up into *little* pieces."

Exodus smirks, "Oh yeah, we wouldn't want that," he takes a seat next to us. "I'll get the keycard to you after lights out."

"Sounds good."

The pain encasing my entire body encourages me to ask, "There's an infirmary in here, right?"

Raphael shakes his head, "Nope. Salem is survival of the fittest."

I groan, "How come I was hooked up to IV's when I first woke up? Matthew also told me that the doctors were beginning to think I wasn't going to wake up."

"That prick had a medical staff come in to make sure we didn't die. He wants us to die at his hands, not some car crash that he wasn't even a part of."

Two Saints enter the cafeteria. One of them says, "Get back to your cells for lights out."

The three of us stand, and without another word, we head to our cells. My numb toes remind me of Salem's relentless chill.

Tomorrow night, I'll be out of this place. Then, Matthew's head is mine.

CHAPTER FIVE

The bright lights that illuminate my cell wake me. The door is remotely unlocked, and the electronic hum is strangely soothing to my ears. My face is sore, and my throat is raw from all the blood that I swallowed.

This sucks.

I sluggishly climb out of bed, limping over to the door before pulling it open. It takes a few minutes of hobbling, stumbling, and a bunch of profanity before I find my way into the cafeteria. I'm instantly greeted by Raphael and Exodus.

"You look like death," Exodus says, his pale blue eyes squinting under the bright lights overhead.

"I feel like it, too," I remark, turning to Raphael. "How did everything go last night?"

"Do you want the good news, or bad?"

My heart begins to pump faster, "Good. Give me good."

"Chloe's alive and well. She got all wide-eyed and bushy-tailed when I told her that you were out of your coma and making a decent recovery. She's also very optimistic about tonight."

"What's the bad news?"

"I had to kill the guy viewing the security footage. He was

asleep when I walked in, but after I erased all the footage of me, he woke up. Let's just say it didn't end well."

"Do you think they'll trace it back to you?"

"Doubt it. I switched off all the cameras. Everyone's a suspect, and after what happened yesterday in Yale's office, I don't think he'll accuse us."

"What if he does?"

"Then we're screwed."

His words send my heart sinking into the acid-filled pit of my stomach. The three of us head over to the serving line, and after we get our slop and portions of water, we find an empty table toward the back of the room.

I don't even get to take a bite before a fuss is made.

Warden Yale enters the cafeteria surrounded by an escort of Saints. His eyebrows are creased, his glare promises pain, and his lips are curled into a snarl. Behind him enter two more Saints, dragging Silas in by his feet. He's missing his right middle finger, and his entire face is black and blue.

"Attention inmates!" Yale shouts. "Bring your eyes over to Silas Delgado – a leader of a little gang here at Salem. Last night, he went against my wishes of harming a certain prisoner. I took pity on him, letting him live after sawing a finger of his off and beating his face," he pauses, but his expression remains fierce and punitive. "Since I was so merciful, Mr. Delgado thought it would be fine and dandy to leave his cell after lights out and kill one of my best operatives. Turns out Mr. Delgado here bribed one of my soldiers for a keycard, and that was the source of his escape. The Saint in question has been dealt with, and now it's his turn."

"It *wasn't* me!" Silas yells, his stare desperate yet defiant. "I didn't leave my cell last night, got it?"

"I've kept you alive long enough," Yale says, and with that, he snaps his fingers.

Silas' two escorts drop his feet, immediately turning around, unholstering their weapons, and blasting his face full of bullets.

Yale grimaces, "The next inmate who tries to act out like our friend Silas here will meet the same fate, do I make myself clear?"

Every inmate audibly agrees. Yale and his escorts leave, two of them dragging Silas' body out of the musky, bright cafeteria – the air reeks of pocket change.

Raphael grins the second they're gone, "Well, I guess we're in the clear, boys."

I let out a sigh of relief, "I think you're right."

The two Saints that stand guard at the cafeteria doors order us all to get in a line. We comply, getting in formation before the two of them make their way down the line and assign jobs.

"Laundry," one says to Raphael.

"Kitchen," the other says to Exodus.

The first soldier side steps in front of me, "Toilets."

I groan, but he ignores me and moves over to the next prisoner. After the rest of the inmates are assigned a job, our escorts take us our separate ways. Today, I'm cleaning cell block two with sixteen others.

Like clockwork, the second we get set up our escorts leave.

I begin scrubbing my assigned toilet.

Tonight's the night. It becomes my mantra.

Despite only hearing about this plan yesterday, I feel confident in its success. Raphael and Exodus have been planning this for who knows how long. I'm excited, not nervous. I'm only worried about my legs and if they'll hold up during our departure. If I can't effectively walk, how am I going to climb down a penitentiary?

Don't worry. It's all going to work out just fine.

I wonder if Lazarus is still operating and pursuing Matthew. If they're all wiped out, will that lessen my chances of killing him?

It better not.

Something out of the corner of my eye causes me to stop scrubbing. I look over, and my heart stammers at the sight of my best friend, a smile present on his face, his throat absent of a gaping wound.

"Si—Simon?" I utter. The words scrape out of my mouth.

"Orange was never a good color on you," he says. Strands of black hair peek out from under his familiar beanie.

My bottom lip trembles as it curls into a half smile, "Screw you too."

He chuckles, stepping a bit closer to me, "You need to get out of this hellhole."

"I'm working on it."

"Stay focused, oh, and you missed a spot."

I glance down, seeing crusted puke stuck to the side of the toilet bowl, "Thanks."

"No problem, you schizo."

I flip him off allowing a laugh to escape from my lips, "Piss off."

I know he's just a fragment of my shattered mind, but I welcome it.

He cracks his knuckles, "One last thing."

"What?"

"You're about to get a killer headache."

"Huh?"

My vision dips in ink as something crashes into the back of my head. I slump forward, banging my nose against the toilet's rim.

CHAPTER SIX

My eyes open. Above me, I recognize the only source of light is a dangling bulb hanging from the ceiling. My hands are tied behind my back, and I'm slumped on a cold, stone floor with freezing drool pooling around my face.

I get on my knees, noticing that Chloe and Raphael flank me. Chloe's tears streak down her cheeks, and Raphael looks furious. His lips are pressed, his eyebrows are slanted, and his stare is the embodiment of rage.

I turn my focus to the front and see Matthew fringed by two Saints.

My blood boils over.

"Good evening, Jason," my murderer greets. His one good eye is wide with sick pride. "Sleep well?"

I glare and force sound between my clenched teeth, "Kill yourself."

He ignores me. He flexes his hands and clasps them behind his back, "Since our meeting a few weeks back, I've made a lot of progress. All of Lazarus is dead. Well, most of them anyway," he pauses, a wicked grin sweeping across his face. "Now, it's your turn."

He pulls a pistol out from behind his back and aims it at my face.

I show no sign of fear, instead I bare my teeth, "How's your daughter?"

His expression twists into a mask of hatred and antipathy, "*What* did you just say?"

I don't answer. He extends his trigger finger, but a loud and powerful knock startles him.

He turns toward the disturbance, foaming at the mouth, "*Who the hell is it?*"

The voice that comes in return is unforgiving, firm, old, yet exhausted, "It's Mills."

An eerie silence encases the room. Matthew blanches, and from outside the barred-up window to my right, a wickedly-timed flash of lightning illuminates the entire room, sending a chill down my spine.

Joseph Mills. Our autarch.

Matthew looks over at his men and orders them to unlock the door and open it. They do as they're told. The metal blockade is moved back on its hinges, and two Reapers swiftly enter, shoving the soldiers to the side.

"Make way for the president," one says, his voice modulated through his mask.

Deep and metallic.

The two Saints back up to separate sides of the room. The Reapers step out of the way to let Mills enter.

He looks weathered. His face is creased with wrinkles, his hair is the color of salt and pepper, and his dead eyes are a faded brown. He has a golden cane gripped in his right hand despite not looking to need it.

"Mr. White, I thought we discussed this?" he mutters as more flashes of lightning illuminate the room. His pristine black tuxedo and his polished dress shoes are shockingly out of place.

Matthew takes an unsteady breath, "Well, yes, sir."

"Why are you holding a private execution behind my back?"

"I – I wasn't."

"Oh really?"

"Well—,"

"You wouldn't lie to me, would you?"

Matthew's gaze lowers, "I wanted to be the one to do it."

"I see," Mills pauses for a moment. "But as you know, it doesn't matter what you want, Matthew. It matters what needs to be done. A private execution won't solve anything. They're doubting me! We can't have any more complications come up with such little time left!" he stops, calming himself, the hand that grips his cane trembles slightly. "That's why I want the three of them brought to the Estate tomorrow morning. There, I'll have the pleasure of decapitating them in front of millions and millions of my subjects, demonstrating my strength."

My left eye twitches, and my fists quake behind my back, "You *sick* bastard."

Mills finally looks at me as more lightning surges through the gloomy sky outside of Salem's thick walls. "Prisoner 31103. You've been a thorn in my side long enough. No matter, though. You'll be headless by the time the sun reaches its peak tomorrow," he brings his attention back over to Matthew. "Have them loaded up tonight. It's a thirteen-hour drive to Seattle. And remember, I want the three of them there by dawn."

Matthew nods, "Yes, sir."

Mills turns around and begins to walk out the door, but stops short, "Oh, and Matthew?"

"Yes, sir?"

"I will deal with your disobedience after the three of them are dead."

Mathew stands silent for a second, then mutters, "Understood."

Mills and his Reapers leave, letting the large metal door shut behind them.

One of the Saints looks over at Matthew, "What now, sir?"

Matthew ignores him, stepping over to me and whipping the side of my face with his gun, forcing my head to reel to the side, "That's for Annie."

The pilot light of anger flares up into a bonfire within my chest, and I lunge into Matthew and take him to the floor, slamming my forehead into the bridge of his nose.

"You stupid little kid!" he blurts, using his hands to keep my head away.

"I'm going to kill you!" I yell. I bite down on his right thumb, crunching down as hard as I possibly can before yanking the detached flesh and bone away from his hand and spitting it out onto the floor.

He screams, throwing me off of him and onto the chilled cement. The two Saints hurl their boots down on me, snapping my nose out of place.

Raphael creeps up from behind, twisting one of the soldiers' neck to the side before tossing his body to the floor. The other one turns around, but Raphael has already got his hands on the fallen Saint's shotgun and shreds the attacker's face apart with a single pull of the trigger.

I purge my mouth of the blood pooled inside, but the sound of the entrance opening and shutting forces me to look.

Raphael blasts the door full of pellets right as it shuts, swearing.

Glancing around, I see that Matthew's gone.

"You should've finished him off!" I growl, blood staining my teeth.

"I tried," Raphael retorts, grabbing me by the collar of my jumpsuit and hoisting me up to my feet. He turns me around and breaks my restraints. "I was a bit busy saving you, like always."

I wipe my nose across my forearms, picking another shotgun from up off the floor, "Thanks."

I lean over and weakly help Chloe to her feet. She lets Raphael undo her restraints, "What now?"

The deafening sound of Salem's escape siren blares into the air, and red lights flash overhead.

I spit some more blood onto the floor, "We fight our way out of here."

CHAPTER SEVEN

My ears ring as a blast of pellets bursts from the barrel of my shotgun and into the face of the soldier charging directly at me. His lifeless body collapses to the cold cement floor.

Chloe, Raphael, and I have no cover, and more and more Saints storm down the corridor.

I think I'm running out of shells.

"We need a distraction!" Raphael blurts, squeezing the trigger of his firearm and ripping a Saint's shoulder apart, forcing him to cry out. "And we need one fast!"

More Saints storm down the tight hallway, their guns trained on us. My adrenaline spikes, and I blast one of them in the chest, sending him to the floor. One of them shoots at us, grazing Chloe's wrist.

She screams.

I begin to panic, my ears reverberating as Raphael kills the soldier, then another. He looks over at the door to our right, then pauses, the corridor ahead of us littered in corpses.

"Wait here," he says, walking over to the door and opening it, revealing a stairwell. "I know where we are. The security room is just up ahead."

"What are you planning?" I ask, checking my shotgun's chamber to see if there's a shell loaded in. There is.

"Just trust me," he enters under the doorway. "I'll only be a couple of minutes."

I nod, and he disappears out of sight, the sound of bare feet on metal steps echoing throughout the strip.

I take a moment to assess Chloe's condition. Blood drips from her fingertips. She's wincing, and her gun lies on the floor.

"We need to get you patched up," I say; the chiming in my ears is maddening.

"I'll be fine. I just need a moment."

"You're looking really pale."

"I've always been really pale."

I hear feet stomping in the distance, and even through all the ringing, I know they're getting closer.

I silently tell Chloe to drop to the floor and play dead. She tilts her head in understanding, and the two of us drop to the floor, my shotgun gripped loosely in my hands.

Four Saints storm the hallway; their guns at the ready. They stop when they see the numerous bodies littered before them.

"Who exactly are we dealing with?" one asks. Each step takes him further down the corridor.

"Lazarus. Didn't you pay attention to the briefing a few weeks back? Prisoner 31103 and his partners are the ones who breached Fort Allister some months ago," the one to his left says.

"That was them? I thought Prisoner 31103 was just some nobody who screwed up big time?"

They all pause, seeing me and Chloe sprawled out across the cold floor.

"No way." one says, looking over to his three buddies. "That's them."

I take slow shallow breaths, hoping they don't notice.

My finger slowly grips the trigger of my gun.

"Call it in," one orders. "Tell Yale that Prisoner 31103 and Prisoner 31209 are both dea—"

I quickly aim the barrel up at his head and pull the trigger. He buckles to the floor.

"Kill him!" one of the remaining three orders.

I attempt to chamber another shell, but I'm out. The Saints aim their weapons, but Chloe grabs her gun and shreds one of their legs apart. She fires another shell, this time hitting the same soldier in the throat.

I kick the Saint in front of me in the upper shin, and he screams as the blood-curdling crack of his kneecap snapping out of place echoes in the hall. The last Saint aims down at Chloe, but I chuck my gun at him, hitting him in the side of the face, causing him to stumble.

Chloe aims at him and fires.

The Saint who just broke his kneecap is on the floor, begging for us to leave him alive.

"What do we do with him?" Chloe asks, trying to avoid looking at the mutilated soldiers around her.

I gradually stand, my legs straining in agony. I look down at the wounded Saint, "The last time I let one of your kind live, he shot me through the back and got a little girl killed."

He cringes in pain, staring up at me with defiant brown eyes, "You're no different than us."

My nostrils flare, and I let out a little chuckle, my expression pained and angry. *Is he right?* I reach over and pull the mask off his face, turning to Chloe and wrapping the black fabric around her wound. I look back to the solider, grab his gun from up off the floor, and swipe it across his face. He blacks out.

We're nothing alike.

Salem's siren is cut, leaving a peculiar hush to linger in the air; Chloe and I exchange looks, and Raphael's voice interrupts the quiet.

"Ladies and gentlemen," he says, his voice filled with charisma. "it's time to riot."

His voice is replaced with a monotoned pre-recorded man announcing that every cell and door in Salem has been opened.

A grin breaks across my face, but it quickly fades as the pain surges throughout my lower body.

I ask Chloe, "Is the mask helping with the bleeding?"

"I can't tell. Let's just be happy that I wasn't hit up close."

I agree, and she drops her firearm, telling me that it's empty before picking a handgun from up off the floor. She takes a fast glance at the maimed face of one of the soldiers, puking all over the floor seconds later.

I step back, not wanting to be splashed with vomit.

After she's done, she looks over at me, wiping her mouth with the back of her hand, "Ah, that's disgusting."

"Come on," I say, limping my way down the corridor, "let's go."

"What about Raphael?"

"He'll catch up to us."

She nods, striding to my side. Her blonde hair is matted in blood, her face is as white as snow, and her emerald green eyes shimmer with tears from all the pain. She's maintained her figure. Her hair is a little longer; It's grown down past her shoulders.

"When we get out of here, you definitely need to hit a drive-thru," she tells me, and I chuckle.

"You're saying I'm too skinny?"

"Well, yeah. That's to be expected when you're in a coma for four months."

"Touché."

She grimaces as I tighten the fabric around her wound.

I hear a door open behind us. Raphael and Exodus jog down the hall with smirks plastered to their faces.

Chloe and I wait for them to catch up.

"You bit off a dude's thumb?" Exodus asks me.

"Focus," I say. "What's our next step."

"Well, I think we need to go with our original plan and climb down Salem."

"Are you insane, dude? I don't think I can even climb down a flight of stairs, let alone a five-story building in the rain. My legs are screwed. We need to find another way."

Exodus turns to Raphael, "What time is it?"

He shrugs, "I think one of the security monitors said it was ten-thirty."

"Okay, good, that means the cargo boat should still be here."

Chloe chimes in, "I'm sure they'll be long gone after they get word that there's a riot in progress."

"She's right," I agree. "We need to get out of here, and fast."

"We could always join the other inmates and riot our way out of here," she suggests, her teeth grinding, tears streaming down her face. She doesn't allow the pain to reach her voice. I admire her strength. She steadily continues, "Or would that be too risky?"

Exodus shakes his head, "No, that would be a death sentence. I can pretty much guarantee that every prisoner who's rioting right now will be shot and killed," he pauses, looking over at me. "There's no other way out of here. We need to climb down."

I grit my teeth, "I told you already, I can't."

"Listen, would you rather take your chances climbing down Salem, or be left here to be found by a bunch of Saints who are more than willing to kill you?"

"Neither. I just—"

"Listen, Pinder," Raphael says, his shotgun loosely held in his hands. "There's no other way."

Chloe touches my hand, "I'll make sure you make it down to the ground without falling; trust us."

I hesitate, but eventually submit, "Fine."

CHAPTER EIGHT

We make it to the barracks, sticking to the shadows and avoiding conflict. Since Raphael remotely unlocked every cell and door inside Salem, we're able to quietly open the entrance to the garrison.

We're all shocked to see that it's empty, absent of life, and quiet.

Exodus pushes the door open the rest of the way, ushering us inside, "That's convenient. I was thinking they'd all be held up in here like last time."

Chloe raises an eyebrow, "If you thought a bunch of soldiers were standing behind this door, then why did you take us?"

He shrugs, "It's the only access route to the roof."

I turn to him, "If they aren't here, then where are they?"

"Dealing with the riot in progress," Raphael assures, scanning the area back and forth with his eyes.

I can hear hushed whispers in the distance. Raphael, Exodus, and Chloe pause, listening to the quiet voices. We all hold still; our breathing becomes shallow and silent.

"You have to get off this island, captain, do you understand?" the voice orders.

Exodus' eyes widen, and he rushes off toward the source, motioning us all to follow him. We all park outside an opened office door. Exodus peeks inside, and his expression hardens.

He dashes inside the room, and the three of us watch as he slams Warden Yale's face down onto a keyboard.

"Hang up the phone!" he demands.

"Okay, okay," Yale blurts, immediately ending the call. "Please, just don't hurt me!"

Exodus forces Yale's face up off the keyboard, and with gnashed teeth, he orders him to call the captain back and tell him to stand his ground.

"You're *insane!*" the Warden yells, a trail of blood streaming from his left nostril.

Exodus hurls Yale's face back down onto the keyboard, raises it up, then slams it down again, "Do it! Do it, or else I'll bash your head into nothing but a bloody mess!"

Yale gulps hard, reluctantly complying by dialing the captain back. Exodus lets him go.

"Sir?" a voice on the other end greets.

"Yes, hello. I need you to stand your ground. We have the riot under control."

"Are you sure?"

Yale glances over at Exodus' glare, "Yes. Yes, I'm very sure. I'll send out a few soldiers after everything calms down to retrieve the shipment."

"Understood."

Yale hangs up, "There, I did what you ask, now let me leave."

Exodus snarls, "Say hi to my dad for me."

"Wait, no, I did what you—"

I watch as he slides a shank out from his jumpsuit sleeve, jabbing its jagged tip into the side of the Warden's throat. Yale's eyes go wide. His suit changes to a darkened color as the liquid from his throat is absorbed through the fabric.

Exodus tosses him to the floor, "Adieu, old man."

I enter the room with Raphael. Chloe follows.

"Good work," Raphael says, admiring the dead body on the ground.

Exodus ignores him, stepping over to the keyboard and pressing numerous keys. The monitors mounted up on the wall go blank, and after pressing a few more keys, he informs us that he's disabling the cameras and deleting all of the footage.

"I'm guessing that's the hatch that leads up to the roof?" Chloe asks, pointing up at the trap door over in the corner of the room, a ladder leading up to it.

"Yep," Exodus steps away from the desk, making his way over to the ladder. "Come on."

The four of us climb up to the roof. I go last, eyeing the dead corpse behind me as I ascend the ladder. The moment the cool, wet breeze hits my face, my stomach drops. The night has just begun, and the thought gives me the urge to vomit.

"This is going to suck," Exodus says, lightning illuminating the sky and rain pouring from the heavens.

We scamper across the flooded rooftop, stopping at the edge.

I stare down at the ground that's over a hundred feet away. The sheer size of Salem is intimidating enough. Rain immerses the scene, and my breathing tightens at the thought of slipping.

"I can't do this," I mutter, and off in the distance the sound of gunshots bounce between the myriad of buildings that I had no idea existed on the island; a greenhouse, a couple of small brick buildings, and a lighthouse near the dock with its blinding light rotating around the perimeter. "There has to be another way."

Chloe puts her hand on my shoulder, rubbing it with her thumb in order to soothe me, "We won't let you fall. If your legs start to give out, just call for help."

I snort, "I don't think you understand; that car crash left me with a twisted body that doesn't want to cooperate at all."

Raphael's soaked bangs partially obscure his right eye, "As long as you rely more on your upper-body strength instead of your lower, you'll be fine. Lazarus taught you how to do crap like this – prepared you for situations where you're completely screwed."

The gunshots sound closer, and I know we have to move. I take one last look down the side of the building and my heart bursts, my legs wobble, and my mind swims in and out of focus.

"Let's get this over with."

CHAPTER NINE

Rain drenches my body, my fingers won't stop cramping, and my legs are useless.

A swear escapes my lips. I let go of one of the window seals and fall to another ledge eight or so feet below. I'm about to plummet past it, but I grab onto the wet ledge and hold on with all the strength I have left.

"You good, Pinder?" Raphael asks in a hushed tone, a few ledges below me.

I swear some more, wanting to flip him off for making me do this, but I don't dare let go, "Y-yeah."

My biceps are burning, begging me to let them rest, but I can't. I let myself drop again, barely catching myself on another ledge. This one's even more slippery.

My fingers begin to slide; the cramping and wet surface are too much for them to handle.

No, no, no!

The word help forms in my mind but doesn't make it to my lips before I reluctantly let go, falling past a few more ledges. Miraculously, I am able grab onto one. The sudden force is so jarring that I feel my left shoulder pop out of place, forcing a brief scream to pass through my lips. The pain is so sharp and abrupt that I almost let go again, but the adrenaline pumping through me forbids it.

"Jason!" Chloe calls out, sheer panic in her voice. "Jason, don't let go!"

I let my left-hand fall, the shoulder unquestionably dislocated. I hang on tight with my right and refuse to drop, rain streaming down my face, pain surging throughout my entire body.

Tonight's a bad night to be a lefty.

I glance down, the ground is about twenty-five feet away.

I'm almost there. The fall wouldn't kill me.

Raphael drops down to the ledge next to mine. Unlike me, he's managed to keep his strength in this cesspit.

"Here," he says, leaping over to my ledge and grabbing on next to me. "Get on my back, I'll take you the rest of the way."

"No, I've got this," I say, even though it's an obvious lie. "Just keep an eye on me. I dislocated my shoulder."

"I'll pop it back into place when we hit the bottom."

"Thanks."

He glances up. I follow his gaze, and standing right behind the window just inches above us is a Saint. He's peering outside, a fully automatic machine gun in his hands. Two more soldiers appear at his side, and then my right-hand cramps up and I have no other choice but to let go. The fall only lasts a second before Raphael grabs my hand – my left hand.

I scream in agony as surges of pain spark up my forearm and into my fingertips. My vision burns white. Raphael's eyes go wide, and the three soldiers immediately look down. They aim their weapons at us and fire.

The sound of glass shattering and gunshots fill my ears as Raphael and I plunge to the earth below. It's over within three seconds; the impact knocks the wind out of me, leaving me unable to breathe.

I don't have time to think before I'm grabbed by my good arm and dragged over to the base of the prison, Raphael tells me not to make a sound. I obey, still fighting to breathe, my left arm hanging loosely at my side and dragging across the wet grass.

"Prisoner 31103 is outside of Salem. I repeat, Prisoner 31103 is outside of Salem! Send all available troops to the yard and apprehend him!" a soldier above orders.

Raphael pulls me to my feet, and my lungs flutter back to life.

"This is gonna hurt like hell," he says.

I clench my teeth, a low-pitched growl escaping my lips as he resets my shoulder. The audible crack reverberates inside my ears. The pain in my shoulder instantly subsides, and I sigh. I can then feel my tailbone stinging from the fall.

Chloe and Exodus drop down next to us.

"We've gotta go!" Exodus demands.

I wrap my arm around Raphael, and he helps me follow Chloe and Exodus as they sprint off toward the docks. My legs don't cooperate, so he ends up hauling me along with him, my feet dragging across the yard.

The boat isn't that big; it looks like it's only meant to fit a handful of people and a few shipments of cargo which it holds tied down in the back.

Raphael hands me off to Exodus, who props his forearm underneath my armpit and keeps me upright.

"Let's load up," Chloe says.

Raphael tilts his head to the side, "Where's the captain?"

Exodus groans, "We don't have time for this. Come on."

The four of us climb on the boat. Exodus sits me down on a wooden bench that's underneath the little roof covering the cab.

For a military transport, it's cheap and old; it's fit for a bunch of fishermen.

Raphael sits down behind the steering wheel, turns the keys, and listens as the motor roars to life.

"Hey!" someone calls out. "That's my boat!"

The four of us watch the captain rush at us with a pistol gripped in his hand.

Exodus sprints off toward him. The captain raises the gun, but Exodus closes the gap too quickly and the captain gets tackled to the dock. Exodus throws his knuckles into the man's face over and over again, blood staining his fists before tossing his unconscious body into the ocean.

The short burst of an alarm goes off, the front gate to Salem opens, and a sea of Saints hurry out.

"Come on!" I blurt, motioning Exodus over to us.

He nods, running back to the boat and hopping on before Raphael speeds off.

We don't get too far when the bullets start whizzing past our escape vessel.

I throw Chloe to the ground and shield her with my body as the boat is riddled with bullets. Shrapnel flies everywhere, and a chunk slices the side of Exodus' thigh open. He cries out. From my cover, I see a midnight black assault rifle lying underneath the bench.

I leave Chloe vulnerable, diving to the floor and grabbing the gun. More bullets shred the cab as I grip it in my hands; it's heavy, yet comfortable. Images of my training flash through my mind, and a little grin makes its way across my face. I sluggishly get to my feet. After taking a deep breath, I peek the gun over the side of the boat and pull the trigger. Flashes from the muzzle obscure my sight as I spray the docks. My shoulder throbs with each kick of the gun.

I love this feeling.

After emptying the magazine, I toss the gun to the floor. We're too far now for them to get a good shot, so I take a deep breath, limping over to the shredded bench to find a seat. The salty spray from the ocean spews everywhere.

Chloe gets to her feet, unharmed, relieved, "We. . . We actually did it."

Exodus sits next to me, his right leg soaked in blood. He's speechless, unable to get a single word out. He's been trapped inside that place for years, and now he's finally out. He's out.

"Do you think they've contacted the Saints stationed in San Francisco and alerted them about the riots?" I ask Raphael, who's concentrated and focused on the path ahead of him.

"Nope. When I cut the sirens and released all the prisoners, I disabled all communications."

"But what about Yale?" Exodus asks. "He got in contact with the captain."

"That was his personal cellphone. So, unless they contacted the Saints on the mainland with their own phones, they'll be unaware."

I look at the mainland a little over a mile away. The city lights shine bright through the rain, and the fact that I'm actually free makes me feel euphoric.

"So," Chloe starts, her natural color returning to her face; the makeshift bandage wrapped around her wrist must be doing its job. "What now?"

"Wait until we dock," Raphael says. "They could have the boat rigged with mics."

I look up, and unsurprisingly, there's a tiny camera placed in the corner on the ceiling. "Yeah, he's right."

Exodus and Chloe look up at the camera. Exodus stands up, blood steadily dripping down his leg as he picks the empty gun up off the floor, walks over to the unwanted device, and bashes it into fragments.

"You don't look so good," Chloe says, eyeing his wound. "You're bleeding pretty bad."

He chuckles, tossing the gun to the floor, "Look who's talking," he pauses, limping back over to the bench before sitting down. "How's your wrist? What even happened?"

"Shotgun blast. Just a graze, though."

"A graze? That mask wrapped around it is soaked in blood."

"I'll be fine."

"How'd you even climb down Salem?"

Chloe snorts, leaning up against the wall by my side, "You haven't met anyone from Lazarus before, have you?"

"Nope," Exodus replies. "Not before you three."

Raphael interrupts, "You know they're going to follow us, right?"

"Well, duh," Exodus laughs. "That's why we're ditching the boat the second we dock."

Raphael nods, and we let the sounds of the waves and rain engulf our insecurity. Thunder rumbles the sky, rain continues to pour down. We allow the feeling to wash over us; the four of us are free.

I take one last look at Salem; at its ancient lighthouse, looming guard towers, spotlights, charred black walls, and the statues of Mills soaring high into the sky. Matthew's there right now with his missing thumb, his dignity gone, but that's only just the beginning of his suffering.

I should've just left him dead back in Brookhaven so many months ago, but I didn't. I was too selfish, too caught up in wanting to get even.

I don't want to get even, anymore. I desire more than that. I want to damage him more than he ever damaged me.

CHAPTER TEN

After docking, we ditch the boat and run. We run until we're heaving, retching, and completely out of energy. My legs hurt so bad, but I don't care; I can't risk getting caught again. I can't risk losing what little I have left.

We eventually stop in the middle of a small grove of trees. I collapse to my knees, puking all over the grass. I hold still long enough to feel my shins throbbing, my shoulder aching, and the fire in my lungs.

My skin is numb from all the rain. My jumpsuit is tattered, muddy, and bloody from being beaten back in the execution chamber.

"No way they're finding us," Exodus pants, spitting mucus.

I breathe, "Good, because I need to rest."

Chloe looks at me, "I'll go find some us some supplies. There's gotta be some clothes and first aid—"

"No way," I interrupt. "You're not going alone, not with your wrist all torn apart."

"I'm fine. You obviously can't come with me, and neither can Exodus; you two are both injured."

"I can go with you," Raphael suggests.

"No, you need to stay here in case any Saints wander over."

Exodus nods, "She's right."

Chloe shoots me a smile, "I'll be fine."

"Yeah," Raphael agrees. "We need the supplies. One of us has to go, and Frye's the quickest."

I slide to a nearby tree, leaning up against its trunk, "But what if you get caught? It's way past curfew and there's probably Saints patrolling everywhere like usual."

"So?" She asks. "I'm not some damsel in distress, Jason."

I sigh, "Okay, okay, fine. Please, just be safe."

"I will," she approaches me before kneeling down. "Get some rest."

My chest is swept with warmth as she presses her lips against mine, and all the memories of her and I before Salem come flooding in to comfort me further. She's the only one who makes me feel this way, but knowing that I have to focus on the events happening now, I brush them away.

"I'm a size thirteen," I say the moment she parts from me.

She raises an eyebrow, "Huh?"

"My shoe size. It's thirteen . . . if you bring me back some sneakers, I'll love you forever."

She laughs, and Raphael tells her his shoe size.

"What about you?" she asks Exodus.

He looks at her like she's crazy, "I haven't worn shoes in like five years. Just take a wild guess, but honestly, I couldn't care less if you bring me back a pair or not," he pauses. "What you can do, though, is get me some shades."

"Shades? You want sunglasses? It's not even light out."

"I've got eye problems. Any bit of light hurts."

"Oh, gotcha. I'll see what I can do."

We all say goodbye, and she leaves.

"So, now that we're in the clear," Raphael starts, leaning up against a tree. "We need a plan. We need to find Vice."

"Vice?" Exodus asks.

"Leader of Lazarus."

"Oh."

I close my eyes and listen to the rain pelting the leaves above, "You sure he's even alive?"

"Explain?"

"Matthew said you and Chloe sung like birds."

He goes silent, and he doesn't speak for what seems like minutes, "He played with my head, Pinder. Put me under hallucinatory drugs for weeks at a time. He ripped my fingernails off, beat me with a hammer, and threatened to take my eyes out. Two months . . . for two months this went on, and I was trying so hard not to crack. The pain was nothing; pain is just an illusion. It's only there to tell you that you're being damaged. . . it was the mind games. He got me so doped up that I couldn't tell dreams from reality, and eventually, he got everything he needed."

His words pry my eyes open, "What did you tell him?"

"All about Rebirth, where it's stashed, and where all our major facilities are; names, appearances, everything."

"Gnarly," Exodus mutters.

"Get some sleep, you two," Raphael orders. "I'll wake you if anything happens."

I nod, closing my eyes once more. Raphael's story of his torture makes me feel squeamish. I imagine his fingernails being pried off, and the blood dripping onto the floor. I imagine a hammer being bashed into the side of his face. Most of all, though, I imagine the mind games.

Sleep catches up, and my mind goes blank.

⚬

I WAKE TO RAPHAEL SHAKING ME. HIS EYES ARE WIDE, and the look on his face immediately alarms me.

"What?" I ask, rain still splashing from above. "What is it?"

He moves his lips, but the sound of gunshots answer for him.

They're coming from the city just a mile away. At first, it's just a few, but more and more sound off.

Chloe.

I get to my feet, and Exodus does the same. Without any other words exchanged, we run toward the sound of gunfire. The sudden adrenaline pouring into my bloodstream keeps my legs from hurting too bad. We run for at least seven minutes before we reach the massive city of San Francisco. Buildings tower overhead, stop lights go from red, to green, to yellow, and back again. A slight fog hangs in the air.

"Where are we going?" Exodus asks, the gunshots having been quiet for a couple of minutes.

"I don't know," Raphael replies.

My stomach knots up, and the sound of screeching tires break loose from the next street over. The three of us run to the street corner, and my blood turns icy cold.

Chloe lies on the ground surrounded by a patrol of Saints. They're taking turns kicking her, and I'm about to mindlessly rush in, but Raphael pulls me back, telling me to calm down.

"We can't just leave her there," I argue, my teeth clenched, my eyes wide.

"We aren't. Look over at the patrol car," he demands.

I glance over. The driver-side door is opened, and lying on the seat is a handgun along with a knife.

Chloe's screams pull my attention, and I see one of the Saints pinning her to the road.

I get ready to sprint over to the car, but again, Raphael pulls me back, "Listen, Pinder, you'll get killed. Your legs are ruined, your shoulder was just reset, and you were beaten by a bunch of soldiers. Exodus and I will take care of them."

"Then hurry," I growl, and I watch helpless as the two of them sneak over to the car, avoiding any eyes. Raphael grabs the gun, and Exodus grabs the knife.

Exodus makes the first move, silently rushing behind one of

the Saints and slicing his neck open. Disturbing images of Simon flash through my mind, but the sound of a gun going off snaps me out of it. Another soldier collapses to the ground, and Raphael fires again, sending a bullet into the face of another Saint.

A bloody fight breaks out, and I watch the two rapidly kill the patrol, the element of surprise being their only upper hand.

I hurry out from behind the corner and approach Chloe. Her nose and mouth are bleeding, and the new clothes she wears are soaked from the rain.

"Are you okay?" I ask, the adrenaline wearing off. "What happened?"

She grimaces while sitting up, bringing a hand up to her face and wiping the blood from the corners of her lips, "I was going through a closed store when those dicks showed up out of nowhere and started shooting. How did you know where to find me?"

"Raphael heard gunshots," I reply, helping her up.

She cringes as her feet carry her weight, "I think I pulled something."

I open my mouth, but Raphael gets the first word out, "Were you able to get anything for us?"

I nudge Raphael with my elbow and mumble, "Dude?"

She nods, pointing over at a large bag lying across the sidewalk a foot away, "Yeah, hurry and go get dressed. I also found a first aid kit, so I'll help you guys get patched up."

"Nice try," I say. "But we're patching you up first."

CHAPTER ELEVEN

The four of us stand on a sandy shore. The rain has calmed to a mild sprinkle, and the foggy mist is a thick blanket that shrouds the Golden Gate Bridge guarding the bay.

Chloe found me a long white t-shirt along with a dark pair of jeans and white sneakers. Being out of the prison jumpsuit is blissful, and I promise myself that I'll never find myself in one again.

"So," Chloe starts. Her wrist is stitched up and wrapped in gauze. "You actually think Vice is alive?"

"I hope so," Raphael replies with his hands stuffed in his pockets. "because if he isn't, then we're done for."

"Why so pessimistic, man?" Exodus asks. A pair of shades obscures his eyes.

"Think of it this way," Raphael skips a stone across the water. "If Vice is dead, then so are the others. He has more security then you could even believe. So many ways to disappear if things went south. If he's dead, then the others are too, and that's a fact. Without the others, it's just us four versus a blood-thirsty government."

I lean up against a large boulder, craving relief from the pain in my legs, "What happens if that's the case? Are we just going to give up and go into hiding?"

He laughs, "No, Pinder. We'd find another way."

Chloe looks up at the darkened sky, "Yeah, there's always another way."

"Mason Wolfe," Exodus chimes in, and the name gets me to tense up. "Raphael told me about him, and how he told you about some doomsday weapon. What's that all about?"

I recall those memories to my own dismay. That was Simon's last day on Earth.

I flex my jaw while my heart sinks a little deeper into my chest, "It's called the God Code; some biochemical weapon that's supposed to wipe out the population on Christmas Eve. That's all I know."

"Did he tell you where it was located?" Raphael asks. "We haven't had any time to talk about what Wolfe told you."

"No, but there are a few men who have been trusted with its location. I can only remember one of the names, though."

"What was it?"

"Vincent Murdock."

His eyes go wide. Not with fear, but with excitement, "You're kidding me, right?"

"No."

"That's one of Mills' lead engineers. Lazarus tried to take him out a few years back, but he survived the shot to the head; you'd be surprised at how much the human body can handle."

His words give me a sense of direction, "Any idea where he is?"

"Somewhere in New York. That's where most of Mills' elites are."

Exodus picks up a stone and skips it, "Looks like we've got a plan figured out."

"Yeah," Chloe agrees.

The only sound we hear is the timid rain and the occasional

stone jumping across the water. I look at Chloe, and her eyes meet mine. Our eyes are locked for what seems like forever when something rolls next to my feet. I glance down. A small white sphere with a blinking red light on top rests next to my foot.

"Shrapnel grenade!" Raphael blurts.

We dive in separate directions, and the moment I hit the sandy floor, the blast goes off, sending metal shards screaming everywhere. It's over within a second. I look at Exodus. Debris sticks out of him as if he were a pin cushion. Blood streams down his face, staining his shredded clothes red. His jaw is slack, and his eyes are wide.

"Blaine!" Raphael shouts.

Saints storm the grassy hill to our side. They fire their guns as I stand, but they aren't shooting bullets; tiny darts serve as their replacements. One catches me in the neck, and eight pierce my torso; I drop back down to my knees, my vision going fuzzy.

How did they find us?

I collapse to the shore, a salty wave splashing me in the face.

I try to move, but I'm paralyzed.

Abruptly, Matthew appears at my side, one of his hands noticeably wrapped with bandages.

"Light's out," he says, and he kicks me in the face.

Everything goes black.

CHAPTER TWELVE

I awake with a start. Everything is inky black despite my eyes being opened. I try to move my hands, but they're cuffed behind my back. I try to move my legs, but they're also restrained. I feel lightheaded and nauseous. The constant bumps that force my headache to pound, the sharp turns that make me nauseas, and the unforgiving short stops all inform me that I'm in some sort of car.

"Jason," a hushed whisper says to my left. "Jason, are you awake?"

"Chloe?" I whisper back.

"Yeah, it's me. Listen. I think we're on our way to the Estate."

My eyes widen, the words of our President reverberating inside my skull: *That's why I want the three of them brought to the Estate tomorrow morning. There, I'll have the pleasure of decapitating them in front of millions and millions of my subjects, demonstrating my strength.*

I start thrashing around, my teeth clenched, my hands balled up into fists, a low-pitched growl lurching from my lips.

I can't catch a break.

My thrashing grows more violent. There always seems to be

some new sort of twist around every corner; some hellish obstacle thrown at me. When will it end?

"Stop it, prisoner!" A voice orders from up front.

"Piss off!" I yell.

"If you don't stop this second, things will get messy. Last warning."

Reluctantly, I do as I'm told, my chest heaving up and down. I can't breathe. Whatever's over my face is thick and musky, and it's slowly asphyxiating me.

"Jason," Chloe whispers once more. "Calm down, okay? For me?"

I blink, my heart thumping up and down, blood being pumped into every inch of my body.

It's distorted, but I can hear a crowd from somewhere outside the car. They're loud. Venomous sounds emanate from what sounds like a large group of people. I have the feeling they're here to watch me take a sharp blade to the side of the neck until my head's rolling around on the ground.

My fingers twitch in sync with my left eye.

The car abruptly stops. The doors on either side of me open, and I'm pulled from the vehicle and forced to stand on my own two feet.

The crowd encircled around us roars to life as we're moved along. My mind races with too many thoughts. I'm about to collapse to the ground when the man escorting me seizes the honor of throwing me down and forcing me to kneel.

"Welcome, my beloved citizens, to my humble manor!" President Mills greets to the crowd, his voice booming from all around me.

The mob howls in delight.

"Today, I bring to you three members of the horrid organization known as Lazarus!" he continues, his voice laced with poison. "They murder, they destroy, and worst of all, they rebel!"

The crowd boos, throwing derogatory taunts my way.

Brainwashed, little puppets.

"Let me introduce someone I'm sure you're all familiar with," I feel a hand grab a hold of the dark fabric covering my face. "Jason Pinder!"

The sun burns into my eyes. The crowd boo's, and I feel like I'm about to break. A sea of them stand in front of the Reapers who are blocking off accesses to the Estate's front lawn. They all scream at me, telling me to burn in Hell. I just glare in return. My teeth are compressed so tight that they threaten to shatter.

"Next," President Mills, who has a microphone held in one hand, and his cane in the other, says. "we have a young whore named Chloe Frye!"

Fire burns through me, and I watch him pull the black hood from her face. She squints as the light hits her, her emerald green eyes shimmering. She stares defiantly at the crowd, and her bottom lip quivers, but she bites down and flares her nostrils.

There's nothing more I want to do than to kill the coward standing behind her.

Mills side steps over to the last member, but it isn't Raphael or Exodus. The pale, beaten man is only wearing a pair of bloody boxers. His fingernails are missing, and there are deep lacerations littered throughout his body. The only thing obscuring his identity is the black hood covering his face.

"And last," he starts, the microphone up to his sick smile, "but certainly not least, we have the leader of this pathetic terrorist group, Marshal Simmons!"

I watch as the bag is pulled from his head. This is the first I have ever seen him without his infamous metallic morph mask. He has jet black hair, a face paler than my own, and an expression of infamy permanently affixed to his face. Vice. The head of Lazarus.

My ventriloquist.

His brown eyes glance sideways at me. He doesn't speak, and

I'm shocked that he's able to keep such an insolent and hateful look on his face when he's about to be beheaded.

"Any last words, Mr. Simmons?" Mills asks, and my eyes widen as he pulls a shrill blade from out of his cane. The menacing weapon is notched down the sides.

Vice grins at the crowd, "This is only just the beginning, ladies and gentlemen. Lazarus will never fall, and one day soon, your old and fragile leader will meet his demise."

Mills' eyes widen with wrath, his hands trembling, his lower lip twitching. He abruptly swings his weapon back before planting its side into Vice's throat, sending a spray of blood to stain the grass beneath him.

Mills shrieks with pure madness, ripping the blade out and sending it back in. He stops when Vice's head is detached and Chloe is puking all over the lawn.

My stomach churns. This is morbid, inhumane, and soulless.

Mills looks down at Chloe as the crowd roars. Blood stains the white dress shirt beneath his suit coat, "Oh Ms. Frye, how beautiful you look in the setting sun. . . any last words?"

She continues to puke and the red streaks on her face shine bright against her pale skin.

I feel helpless. I want to save her. I want her to make it out of this alive. I can't watch her get beheaded.

"Kill me!" I blurt, my entire body shaking. "Kill me, first!"

Mills' spatter speckled face is in full view. His grin is wide. He pulls the microphone away from his mouth and leans toward me, speaking just loud enough that I can hear over the roar of the crowd. "If you remember correctly, Prisoner 31103, I told you that I'd kill you last so you could see your partners get executed, I hope that you enjoy the show."

A desperate, primal scream explodes from my throat.

"You love her, don't you?"

Vomit rushes out from between my lips, my tongue drowning in acid.

He laughs, swaying his weapon back, readying himself for his next kill.

Chloe looks at me. She mouths something, but my mind is shattered. I can't focus on anything.

Mills swings his blade. It's about to dig inside Chloe's jugular when he jerks back. A bullet flies through his shoulder, spewing blood into the air. He drops his sword, and the Reapers aim their automatic rifles at the crowd and open fire, littering countless onlookers with holes in hopes to kill the shooter.

Chloe jumps to her feet, bashing her forehead into Mills' nose. He collapses, his nose crooked, blood spilling from his nostrils.

A few Reapers get shot in the head by the unknown killer, but the last few turn around, training their weapons on us.

"Kill them!" One orders.

I prepare to get lit up when a black Cadillac speeds onto the lawn, crashing into the elite soldiers and crushing them underneath its wheels.

The tinted window rolls down, and from behind the wheel, Exodus screams at us to get in. Chloe half sprints, half hops over to the car.

I try jumping to my feet, but I crumple back down to the lawn. My legs fail me. From behind, I hear Mills telling me to die.

I stagger out of the way just in time to see the President's sword stab into the grass. He pulls it out, swinging it at me again. I dodge the wisp of the blade as it speeds past my face, sending me into a frenzy.

I kick him in the shin, but that doesn't stop him from swinging again. The blade is about to plant into my skull when a bullet slams into his other shoulder, forcing half his body to lurch back.

Raphael appears at my side, throwing Mills to the ground before grabbing me by my good arm and lifting me to my feet. He half sprints, half carries me to the car. Some Reapers who were busy firing at the crowd aim their weapons at us.

Raphael hurls me into the back seat as the bullets fly. He dives to the ground as one side of the Cadillac is torn apart. One bullet hits my window, and glass flies into Chloe's leg. She yelps, and Exodus screams at Raphael to get in. Before he can shut the door, Exodus has the pedal to the metal.

More bullets penetrate the car as we speed off. Chloe yanks the shard out of her calf, tossing it to the floor, blood oozing from the puncture wound.

We barrel through the security gate, speeding past the Estate's perimeter wall. The vehicle's tires screech as Exodus takes a hard right, leaving our mark down the street.

"How are you even alive?" I ask him, sweat dripping down my face, my breathing unsteady.

"The grenade they threw was only meant to incapacitate its victims. They wanted us alive, and that's what they got," he replies, spinning the wheel counter-clockwise, turning the car down another street.

I stare at Raphael in the front seat. He has a bandana covering his mouth. He's staring down at the gun on his lap, his chest moving up and down rapidly.

"Are you okay?" Chloe asks.

He shakes his head, "Don't talk to me right now, Frye."

I abruptly remember that he just witnessed the decapitation of his father-figure.

I flinch when he rapidly pounds his fists against the dashboard, howling so loud that it scares me. He continues to slam his fists against the car's interior until his knuckles are torn open and bleeding.

I've never seen him like this.

He stops, panting, "We're going to hunt down Murdock, shut down the God Code, and then put Mills' head on a spike for all of America to see. I'm going to piss on his corpse, and I am going to kill everyone close to him."

"Where to now?" Exodus interrupts. The black shades hiding his emotions.

Raphael pulls the magazine out of his handgun, examining how many rounds he has left, "There's an unfinished hotel being constructed a few miles away from here. Turn right."

Exodus does as he's told.

CHAPTER THIRTEEN

It's a chilly, starless night. Raphael and I stand on the edge of the unfinished building's rooftop overlooking Seattle. It's past curfew, so there's no traffic, except the occasional patrol car traversing the streets below.

It's been seven hours since Vice was killed. Raphael and I have been here since reaching the hideout, standing in silence. Neither of us have exchanged a single word. I'm just here to console him.

"We need to bring it back from the dead," he says.

"What do you mean?"

"Lazarus is dead. . . We need to bring it back"

"How?"

He pauses, pondering my words, "I don't know, man."

"You're the leader now," I remark, stuffing my hands inside my pockets. "How do you feel about that?"

He shakes his head, silent once more. We continue to look over the city.

Images of Vice's execution keep flashing behind my eyelids whenever I blink. It was so. . . final.

"Jason?"

"Yeah?"

"You're my new heir."

I'm taken aback, "Me? Why me?"

"Who else? Everyone's dead."

"You don't know that, dude."

"If they got to Marshal, they got to everyone else. It's all my fault. If I didn't break, then they would've never even known who Vice was. They would have gone on thinking he was just some myth, just some urban legend."

"The mind can only handle so much before it shatters."

"You're right, but I should've been different."

We both go quiet again.

"What's the date?" I eventually ask.

"October 10th," he replies.

"The God Code will go off on Christmas Eve. We need to find Murdock, just like you said, and then Mills' weapon. We don't have much time left, and if we don't get this done soon, we're all going to die."

He nods, "You're right, Pinder," he makes his way over to a steel door and turns its knob. "Let's get some sleep so we can start fresh in the morning."

———

I FIND CHLOE IN AN EMPTY ROOM ON THE FIFTH FLOOR. She's staring out one of the windows when I enter, and she turns when she hears the door shut.

"Is he okay?"

"I don't know. I think he just needs some time."

"Yeah."

I park myself at her side, putting a hand on her shoulder, "How are you doing?"

"Cruddy."

"Me too."

She moves away from the window and leans up against a wall,

"This is all just crazy. I mean, how did we even end up in this situation?"

"I wouldn't even know where to begin."

She sighs, stepping away from the wall, unable to keep still, "Can I ask you something?"

"Of course. Anything."

"How do you feel about me?"

I snort, "What type of question is that?"

"Look, I've just been thinking a lot, lately."

"About what?

"I've never really had feelings for anyone before, you know? Sure, little crushes in school and all that, but you've been really messing with me, Jason."

I chuckle nervously. She punches me in the arm.

"I'm being serious."

"I know you are. It's just out of all the things that should be messing with you, I'm one of them."

"Not in a bad way, though."

"Well, if it isn't in a bad way, then what is it?"

She pauses, "I had a lot of time to think back in Salem. We were in there for over four months, and I spent most nights thinking about you. When it was freezing, and hope was long gone, you were my mind's go to."

My cheeks go warm.

She continues, "I know we're supposed to be a part of an uprising, and how we don't have time for *lovey-dovey* crap, but there's something about you that's really special."

"Special? Which part? Me when I wake up from nightmares and sock you in the face, or me when I'm slitting a soldier's throat?"

She rolls her eyes, "You're so hard on yourself."

"Aren't we all?"

She wraps her arms around my neck, and places her head on my chest, "Yeah, but you shouldn't be."

"There's nothing special about me."

She gradually pulls away, looking into my eyes, "You're different from everyone else. You're your own person, and I like that. You're passionate, funny, not to mention a lifesaver."

"Why are you telling me this?"

"Because I want you to return the favor."

I lock eyes with her, "Do you remember what Mills said to me before he was shot in the shoulder?"

"Not really, no. I was a bit busy worrying about having my neck cut into."

"He taunted me; told me I was freaking out because I love you."

"And?"

"And what?"

She laughs a bit, "Stop teasing me."

I chuckle, "You'll never know."

Her emerald green eyes are focused; her gaze is comforting, and it makes me feel calm.

She leans forward and presses her lips against mine. I push her up against the wall, and we continue to kiss. She creeps her hands under my shirt, grabbing a hold of my body. I smooth my hand through her blonde hair, my heart beating like a drum.

I pull away, "He wasn't wrong."

She smiles, leaning back in. Her lips are warm and soft as always.

We don't stop until the door opens. She parts and I turn around to Raphael and Exodus.

Exodus grins, "I see you, Jason. I see you."

"Shut up, Blaine."

"Raphael closes the door, "We need to get some sleep. Tomorrow we're setting off for New York."

"We are?" Chloe asks, fixing her hair.

"Yeah. I feel like it's safer to be all in the same room, so pick a spot and lay down."

We all rush over to the only bed in the room, pushing each other out of the way to get to it. Neither of us have slept on a normal mattress in forever, but in the end, Exodus gets it, which I guess he deserves.

five years is a lot longer than four months.

Chloe and I stick together, picking the corner of the room that has a vent above it blowing warm air. I sit down, leaning my back up against the wall while Chloe rests her head across my lap.

Raphael snatches one of the pillows from off the bed, walking over to the other side of the room.

I close my eyes. The warm air from the vent covers me like a quilt, quieting my mind.

This room full of friends and warmth defrosts Salem's cold grip and I feel like I could be happy again.

CHAPTER FOURTEEN

The sound of footfalls outside the room cause my eyelids to fly open. Chloe's still asleep on my lap, and Exodus is snoring in the bed. My eyes sweep the room, and Raphael's eyes are open, signaling me that he heard the same thing.

"Did they find us?" I whisper.

He nods, silently getting to his feet. He lightly treads over to the door and presses his ear against its wooden surface.

Please just be nothing.

Raphael grits his teeth, moving away from the door and creeping over to me, "It's a soldier. He's on the radio with someone, asking for backup."

"But how?"

"I don't know, but we can't kill him or be seen."

"Why not?"

"A squad of Saints are gonna storm this place within a few minutes. If they find a dead body, they'll know that we've been here – we've gotta get out of here quietly."

I softly shake Chloe awake, and when her eyes focus on me, I press my finger to her lips. She sits up, looking around the room before gazing at Raphael, who's standing in front of us.

"What's going on?" her voice is almost undetectable.

Raphael points over at the door, "There's a Saint in the hotel. He called backup and they're going to search this entire place."

She blanches, immediately getting to her feet, "How did they find us?"

"I don't know, Frye."

I stand, and those familiar jolts of pain shoot up my shins, "Wait here."

The two of them watch as I make my way over to the door. I put my ear against it and listen.

It's quiet for a moment, but then, "Two patrols are in route. White wants to know if there are any signs of life that you can see."

"One of the windows were shattered. Not only that, some of the lights were on in one of the halls."

We're so stupid.

"Copy that. ETA, ten minutes. We're coming armed to the teeth. Those freaks aren't to leave that place alive, got it? And if they do, it's on you."

"Got it. Wilson out."

I pull my ear away from the door, looking over at Raphael and Chloe, "We need to leave now. We only have ten minutes."

Raphael moves to the bed and shakes Exodus awake. His body isn't in good shape; a shard of metal still sticks out of his bicep, gashes litter his face, and dried blood stains his forehead.

He wakes with a start, staring at Raphael, "What? What's going on?"

"The hotel is going to be stormed in ten minutes. We need to get out of here without being seen."

He's bewildered, "What did I miss, dude?"

"I'll tell you later. Just follow us and be quiet."

He nods, getting out of bed and popping his neck.

Chloe puts her ear up to the door and listens.

"What's the quickest way out?" I ask Raphael.

He shrugs, "Same way we came in," he looks over at Chloe. "Do you hear anything?"

She pulls away, shaking her head, "Nothing, not even walking."

"Let's go then."

Raphael gradually opens the door, the hallway outside completely dark. He steps out, and the three of us follow, all voiceless, listening for any sudden noises. We take a left, treading to the stairwell. Raphael instructs Exodus to only walk on his toes the way we learned in Lazarus.

With every creak of the stairs, we cringe, but eventually, we make it to the second floor. The steps leading down to the first are blocked off with construction crap, so we creep down the hallway we have access to.

Shining in through the windows, the full moon lights our way.

"Wait," Raphael stops us. "*Shh.*"

We all pause, listening to the heavy footfalls in the distance.

My eyes widen.

"Hide," Exodus whispers.

"Hide where? There's nowhere else to go. All these doors are locked without a keycard."

"The elevator," Raphael mutters, pointing to the solid steel doors on the right side of the hall.

We all agree, quickly moving over to them before Chloe presses the call button. Less than a second later, the doors slide open. The sound of walking grows closer. We all get inside; momentarily, the doors reunite, leaving us in the cramped cart with faint jazz playing overhead.

We wait for what seems like an eternity before the sound becomes nonexistent, and after another minute of waiting just to be safe, Raphael hits the button for the first floor.

My stomach churns as the cart moves downward.

"We're almost out of time," I say, my legs begging me to stop putting weight on them. "The window we came in from is going to be the first place they check, so I say we just head out the main doors, get back in the Cadillac, and split."

"He's right," Exodus agrees.

The *ding* of the elevator cuts the silence, and the doors open, revealing the lobby and main doors.

Raphael leads us over to the revolving glass entrance, peering outside before exiting. We follow, the cool Autumn wind sending a shiver down my spine.

"Alright, let's go," Chloe says.

The screech of tires breaking loose interrupts our progress. We look over, and my blood freezes as eight patrol cars skid to a halt in front of the hotel.

"Get behind the car!" Raphael shouts, sprinting over to the Cadillac before diving behind it.

Gunshots erupt into the night as the rest of us run for cover. Chloe screams, and I feel something wet splash against my forearm. I don't have time to look, so I blindly grab her by the arm and dive behind the vehicle.

Bullets tear the Cadillac to shreds, destroying the doors, shattering all the windows, and rupturing the tires.

We're screwed.

My eyes bulge at the sight of Chloe. Her hands are pressed up against her stomach, blood soaking her shirt. Her eyes are wide and filled with tears.

"*No! No, Chloe!*" I cry.

She lets her head fall to the asphalt, her hands stained with crimson.

Raphael fires off a few rounds from his gun.

I cradle her, staring down at the blood oozing from her gut. I rip my shirt off, moving her hands away before pressing the fabric down on her wound. She cries out, and more bullets hit the car – one slams into Exodus' chest, knocking him to the ground.

Chloe tries to say something to me, but she can't. I put more pressure on her wound, but this just makes her cry out and wince.

We lock eyes, hers emerald and shimmering with tears. I watch one escape and slide down her left cheek. She breathes, breathes some more, and then nothing.

A bullet slams through the car and penetrates my knee. Another one comes, this time hitting me in my thigh.

I scream.

Exodus breathes out a swear. Blood spills out from his mouth, causing his eyes to bulge out of his skull.

Chloe's face is frozen in saddening confusion. Her chest isn't moving. Tears fill my eyes and spill down my face. I reach up to wipe them away and notice that they aren't bloody. Rebirth's side effect is gone.

That doesn't matter. Not when I'm about to die. Not when she's dead.

Another bullet goes through the car and bursts into my hip. I cry out, lying in a pool of my own blood, mixing with Chloe's.

I'm scared.

I don't want to die.

Another bullet hits me, sending blood flying out my mouth from the sudden impact.

Out of the corner of my inky vision, a white van pulls up, and my eyes widen as two figures pop out, spraying our assailants with bullets, killing each one of them; the Cadillac mostly obstructs this scene, but I still see bodies dropping to the road. I start to feel myself fade from the chaos surrounding me.

The gunfire stops, leaving a peaceful silence in the air.

I feel someone's hand smooth my hair, and I blink through a haze to see my mom smile down at me. I feel blood spill from my lips and blink faster, trying to find reality.

Raphael stands, facing whoever just saved us, "Who the—" he stops, dumbfounded. "Price?"

Tommy and Bleach appear slack-jawed at my side.

Using all the strength I have left, I partially lift myself up off the ground, grabbing onto Tommy's uniform. I try to speak, but I can't; my throat is closing up, and everything feels so heavy.

He looks down at me, "You're going to be okay."

His voice is distorted and distant.

He helps me to my feet, but I crumple the second he lets go.

"I'll carry him," Raphael says, stepping over the gagging Exodus. "You take Frye, and Bleach, you take Exodus."

"That kid on the ground?" she calmly asks.

He nods, bending over and picking me up, "Yeah. I'm guessing those chips you planted in Pinder and Frye's head worked well?"

His words don't surprise me. Nothing does right now. I can only focus on breathing.

Tommy lifts Chloe, "They did their job. Now come on."

Chloe, Exodus, and I are carried over to the van. We're placed in the back, and Tommy quickly injects me with Rebirth.

"Lay back and calm down, she'll be fine," he says, able to read my mind.

Bleach grabs Chloe's limp arm and injects it with Rebirth. I'm flooded with relief, and I allow myself to lie back down. My body feels numb and heavy.

I let my eyes close.

I hear my dad say he loves me.

CHAPTER FIFTEEN

I'm swimming in an ocean of purity. All I see is white. Voices play inside my head, and the occasional memory passes by, pulling me out of the light before dropping me back in, leaving me to drown.

I drown for what feels like an eternity, my thoughts untamable, my body weightless. It isn't until I hear Simon's voice telling me that it's time to open my eyes that a blinding white light flashes me, and a thumping in my chest breaks out simultaneously.

A shudder escapes my mouth as my eyes flash open, my entire body feeling wired. I'm lying on an infirmary bed, and I notice how the room is identical to the one I woke up in months ago.

I sit up, my head spinning.

Chloe sits in a chair at the foot of the bed. She's staring down at a phone, scrolling through something that holds her interest. My chest fills with a warm burst of energy at the sight of her. A moment later, she looks up.

"You're awake," she smiles, standing from the chair. She embraces me, placing her head on my chest. Her hair falls gently across my face.

She looks up, and kisses me. I place my hands on her hips, but she reels back as tears spill from my eyes and trickle down my cheeks.

My vision is blotchy from the blood.

The haemolacria is back.

Rebirth's side effect.

I wipe my cheeks with the back of my left hand, allowing the euphoria to course through me. My legs don't hurt, my body doesn't sting from all the bullets it took, and my shoulder feels amazing.

"How long have I been out?" I ask, glancing down at my bare chest, fresh scars littering the flesh.

"A day. I just woke up a couple of hours ago."

"What time is it?"

"It's noon."

She hands me a Lazarus uniform; I welcome the familiarity that comes with the black hoodie, dark blue jeans, fingerless gloves, and sneakers. There's a difference, though; the hoodie has padding underneath, thin brass underlines the gloves' knuckles, and my jeans have a black holster looped through them. The inside of the jeans are padded as well.

The biggest change of all, however, is the symbol that's etched into the upper chest of my sweatshirt. It's the crude logo I tagged on a brick wall all those months ago the night of my revenge; two creature-like eyes that are set off by a morbid scowl.

I look up at the same symbol on Chloe's hoodie.

"There's been a few changes," she says, catching my stare. "Our clothes have been padded with Kevlar, and I guess Vice really liked your design and had them implemented into the uniform before he died."

"Where's Raphael?" I slip on the attire. "Have you heard from him?"

"He's in New York."

"New York?"

"Yeah. He wasn't injured after the shootout with the Saints, so he flew to New York to find and interrogate that Murdock guy you were talking about back on the beach."

I raise an eyebrow, "Why didn't he wait for us?"

"Something about how *time is of the essence*," she mimics Raphael, then pauses. "Dying feels weird."

"Yeah. . . At least our bodies are all healed up, though," I inhale. "Where's Exodus?"

"He's been in and out of surgery for the last little while."

"What? Why? Wasn't he injected with Rebirth?"

"No, he refused it, and with all the shrapnel stuck in his body and the bullet he took to the chest, he's in rough shape."

"Why'd he refuse it?"

"He didn't want to cry blood, I guess."

"Seriously?"

"I actually don't know. I haven't talked to him."

The door to the room opens and Tommy walks in.

I stand from the bed, and the two of us nod at each other.

"You saved our lives, man."

"I wasn't going to let you die, Jay."

I stop, dread encasing my chest, my heart thumping up and down, "Did you hear about Simon?"

His expression drops, his face tightening, "Yeah."

I nod, and he tells me and Chloe to follow him.

Waves of nostalgia hit me as we step out into the corridor. The white tiled floors, the fluorescent lights built into the ceiling, and the smell of steel feel a bit like home.

"Are we in Boston?" I ask while my shoes pad against the floor.

"Nope. We're in Jersey."

"Jersey? New Jersey?"

"Are there any other Jerseys?"

"Touché."

Chloe speaks up, "Are you gonna tell Jason the news?"

"What news?" my blood is amplified with electricity, and my gaze is focused and determined.

Tommy leads us through a pair of double doors and into a vacant gymnasium, "Almost all of Lazarus is dead. We have about fifty members here, and a couple hundred moles who are out posed as Saints. Things aren't looking good, and we need to act fast if we're going to shut down Mills' biochemical weapon."

The site of the gymnasium causes memories of Fight Night to rush into my mind, "So, let me get this straight. We have, what, two hundred and fifty members left, and you think we still have a chance?"

"Nope, but you're gonna help lead them."

"What do you mean?"

"Raphael informed me that you are his heir."

"That was before we found out that people from Lazarus were still alive. I'm not fit for leadership."

He leads us through another set of doors and into another long corridor, "Not my orders, Jay. Raphael says that you're the only one he wants for the job."

I laugh, "You kidding me? I've been an official member for what? Five months? Me being asleep for ninety-five percent of it. You should get the position, not me."

He shakes his head, snorting, "Nah, I'm good. It's not like we're gonna be alive for much longer anyway. Like I said, practically everyone is dead, and with all the crap Raphael spewed at that prick who's in charge of exterminating us, we don't have much time. The least we can do before taking a dirt nap is save everyone else from genocide."

I grit my teeth, "You can't be serious. You're really giving up because we're down in numbers?"

"You have to be realistic here, Jason. Mills has over six million soldiers at the ready. So do you honestly think we can take him out, kill everyone under him in power, and then off his entire military?"

"Of course, we can," I retort. "Who the hell else?"

"But—"

"But what, Tommy? You just wanna sit back and die when things get hard? We aren't just a bunch of kids who're way in over their head. We're trained killers, we know how to do this. For months and months we've all trained for situations just like this."

"There's no possible way we can still overthrow an entire government with only a couple hundred guys."

"We'll get more. We'll find those who want to start an uprising and train them."

Tommy stops in front of another pair of double doors, turning to me with a grin on his face, "See, I knew you were a good heir."

I stare at him, his words a ruse for me to act like a *leader*, "Wow."

He opens the doors, revealing the large and spacious cafeteria. Each table is occupied by a group of members wearing the assigned attire, and as they look up, I feel sheer excitement.

"This is Jason Pinder," Tommy introduces. "He is the new heir of Lazarus and will be going through training with you all tomorrow morning. Take the rest of the day and use it for some downtime. Go hit the weight room, spar, maybe even take a nap. We're going to let Jason get back in the swing of things, so we'll see you all tomorrow morning in the gymnasium."

All of the members nod, each holding a bold stare in their eyes. They aren't weak; all of them are built and in shape, and each individual looks ready for action.

The three of us turn around and head back through the doors. I can't stop the grin from plastering itself on my face.

CHAPTER SIXTEEN

I throw my bare knuckles into the punching bag, watching it ripple and fly back. I throw a knee, then a punch, and finally an elbow.

My entire body feels that soothing ache that only comes after hours of working out. It's past midnight, and I've spent the day lifting weights and beating the piss out of this poor bag. Both knuckles on my index and middle finger are split open and bleeding, but seeing the blood spattered across the bag fills me with satisfaction. I've been lectured so many times about using my fists in a fight, and how I need to only use my palms, but I love the feeling. It's a guilty pleasure.

I lost almost twenty pounds in that coma. I look weak. I appear fragile. I can't wait until I get back to my normal shape. Tommy said he's putting me on a special training diet and workout plan. He says I'll get back to my desired self within a few weeks. I can only eat fish, chicken, rice, and vegetables and only between the hours of 11:00 a.m. and 7:00 p.m. I also have to work out five hours a day.

I throw a palm into the punching bag, and sweat pours down

my face. I follow my hit with a kick, ecstatic that there's no pain in my legs.

"Hey," Chloe's voice makes me flinch, and she laughs. "Oh, sorry, I didn't mean to scare you."

I chuckle, steadying the bag, "No, you're good. Man, it feels so good to get back to training. I missed it."

"I know, me too," she gazes over at the bag, then at me. "Wanna fight?"

I raise both eyebrows, "Fight? Why? You know I'll beat you."

"Pfft, whatever."

"Don't you remember Fight Night?"

"You got lucky, okay? Plus, I almost beat you, and since you're down a notch in figure, we might as well go at it again. . . that is unless you're scared."

"Scared? You think I'm scared? I'm not scared."

"Well pick up some gloves, then."

I shrug, walking over to a rack and picking up a pair of kickboxing gloves. I slide them on, then toss her a pair. She puts them on, and we both step onto the blue matt next to the punching bag.

"Rules?" she asks.

"No bone breaking, and no mouth shots. I like my smile."

"I like your smile, too," she waits a moment. Then. "Alright, three, two, one, go."

She charges me, throwing a punch. I grab her hands and throw them to the side before kneeing her in the gut. We send and receive strikes from each other, but then she sweep kicks my legs out from under me. Her favorite move takes me down.

My back slams against the ground, deflating my lungs.

She quickly straddles me, pulling her fist back and preparing for the final blow.

I stop her, "Alright, alright, you win."

"What happened to, *'You know I'll beat you.'*"

"I was in a coma for a hundred and twenty days."

"Sounds like an excuse."

"Yeah, a valid one."

She chuckles, leaning in and placing her lips against mine. We're both sweaty and gross, but none of that matters to me. I feel comfortable with her, un-judged. . . normal.

After we part, I look at her with a raised eyebrow, "Rematch?"

CHAPTER SEVENTEEN

My chest heaves up and down, and my calves ache. Sweat trickles down my face.

"Two more laps!" Chloe pants, sprinting ahead of me. Another couple of members do the same.

Warm liquid suddenly rushes up my throat. I bend over, and puke spills from my lips, splattering against the floor, overwhelming my mouth with the taste of battery acid.

Everyone stops and stares at me.

I sputter for air, raising my finger, "Just a moment. . . hold on."

Chloe approaches and leads me to the wall. I lean against the soothing cool foundation, and another member comes up and hands a water bottle to me.

"Thanks," I mutter, spraying some of the cool liquid into my mouth, ridding the acidic taste. "What's your name?"

"Kennedy," he replies, reaching his hand out. "Kennedy Allard."

I spit on the floor, then reach out to meet his grip, "Nice to meet you."

After handing his water bottle back, my eyes meet Chloe's.

She's examining me with a smile on her face, "Slow-poke."

I roll my eyes, wiping my mouth, "Whatever."

She punches me in the shoulder, "I'm just screwing with you."

I straighten my posture, feeling a bit better, "What facility did these members come from? I don't recognize a single face."

Kennedy answers, "From all around. We were all a part of the Beta, just like you two were. I'm from Oregon's facility. You're from Boston's, aren't you?"

"Yeah," I reply, ringing out my sweat drenched shirt. "How'd you know?"

"Your accent."

I raise an eyebrow. *Mine's not even that thick.* "Really?"

He laughs, "No, not really. Everyone's heard of you, man. You went out hanging Saints; torturing, killing, setting houses on fire . . . we were all shown the footage. I was also there in the crowd the night you killed Marcus Terrel. You have a rap sheet, Jason. Everyone here loves you."

I push that night out of my mind, stepping forward, "Alright, everyone! It's time to head to the weight room. We're going to be focusing on core, back, and biceps."

Everyone nods, leaving the gym. I stay behind to clean up my vomit.

※

FRIGID WATER SPILLS FROM THE SHOWER HEAD AND splashes my body. It's been a long day, and since Salem, I've tried to avoid freezing temperatures, but I'm enjoying a sub-zero cleanse, ridding my body of all the sweat.

My fingers pass over the scar etched into my throat. The phantom pain of my first death burns its way into my memory.

I take a deep breath and close my eyes.

There's over thirty scars that litter my body. I stare down at the three seared into my chest, then the one on the back of my hand, I touch each of the multiple raised marks on my hip, my left thigh, and forearm. I remember how I got each one of them and all the pain that accompanied.

Funny thing is, you never get used to pain, no matter how well-known it becomes. It's still an utter shock when it comes barreling in like a freight train.

"Jay!" I hear Tommy blurt. "Jay, you in here?"

"Yeah? What's up?"

"Raphael's dead. We've gotta get to him, and fast."

What. . .?

My eyes widen, my heart pounding, "Are you serious?"

"Yes! Now hurry!"

"Go without me, just go."

"I can't. I need you. Please, Jason, please just hurry."

I turn the water off, grabbing the towel that hangs over the stall and wrapping it around my waist.

No, no you can't be dead. I'm not ready for this. I'm not ready to be the next leader.

I get dressed in such haste that it would've impressed my mom. I slide a handgun into my back pocket and race out the bathroom

CHAPTER EIGHTEEN

The vehicle's engine roars as Tommy spins the wheel, taking us down another backroad. It's been over an hour, which isn't good. Bleach told me that if it goes past the allowed time, that Rebirth won't work.

You can't stay dead. Please, Raph, please don't stay dead.

"Where is he?" I utter the first words this car ride.

"Some park next to an old recycling yard in Queens."

The air is thick with anxiety. My stomach hurts, and my heart is bruising the inside of my chest.

How could he have died? Who could have killed him?

Tommy hits the breaks, bringing the car to a halt.

"What are you doing?" I frantically ask. "We don't have time to waste."

He opens the car door, quickly stepping out, "Look up ahead. There's a checkpoint."

"So? Find a way around."

"It isn't that simple. Look, get behind the wheel, I'm getting in the trunk. Drive up and let me take care of the rest."

I stare at him like he's crazy, "Can't we just—"

"Jason, the park is just a little way from here. If we're gonna get to Raphael, then you need to shut up and do as you're told."

I swallow, fighting the arrogant comments that are yearning to be said, "Fine."

I hop behind the wheel, shut the driver-side door, and adjust the seat. The trunk creaks open, Tommy gets in, and I press a button on the dash that closes it remotely.

I gradually step on the pedal, moving the car forward.

This is suicide.

A few moments fly by before I'm forced to hit the brake. The red and white security gate prevents me from going any further. A Saint stands at attention, staring me down with a narrowed gaze. His buddy steps out from the booth, backing his partner up as he approaches my door.

I roll the window down, and he says, "Step out of the car."

I put on a mask of false panic, "No, sir, you don't understand. My girlfriend–she's having a baby."

The two soldiers scan the vehicle's interior with their eyes, shooting each other befuddled looks.

One of them draws their gun, aiming it at me, "Get out of the car before your *kid* has to grow up without a father."

A noisy bump comes from the trunk, and I leak out some more artificial fear.

"What's in the trunk?" one of the soldiers ask me.

"Please, sir, I—"

He throws the door open, grabbing my arm and shoving me to the ground. He aims his gun down at me, ordering his partner to go check the trunk as another loud thud reverberates from the car.

His partner complies. I listen to the dirt beneath his boot crunch with each step. He opens the trunk, and then both the soldier with a gun to my head and I listen as a struggle ensues. It's quick and ends with a disturbing gurgle.

"Schmitt?" my captor calls out, pulling the gun away from my skull. "Schmitt, you good?"

No reply, just the sound of crickets and the swaying of trees.

He glances down at me before stepping over to the back of the car. I hear him let out a shaky breath.

Tommy creeps past me, shoving a knife into the back of the Saint's neck just as he reaches for his radio.

I get to my feet, popping my neck, "Come on, we need to find Raphael *now*."

He nods, pulling a gun out of his back pocket before pointing it at the lone security camera stalking us. He pulls the trigger and watches it explode into an array of sparks. He holsters his weapon and gets behind the wheel of the car. I hop into the seat beside him.

He presses the gas, and we speed off. He takes a right down another dirt road, and we eventually turn down a main street. A lifeless park rests to our left.

"There he is," Tommy mutters, parking the car on the side of the road.

He jumps out.

Raphael's limp body is sprawled out across the grass. He's wearing Vice's old morph mask. It's current state is crude and charred, the eyes are gaping black holes, and the flexible fabric around his mouth outlines his lips.

I jerk out of the car, sprinting over to his corpse. I stare down at the shredded hoodie covering my friend.

Tommy kneels, pulling a syringe out of his pocket, "Please work," he mutters, jabbing the Rebirth into his forearm before lifting the bottom part of his mask up and shoving a red pill down his throat.

"It's been over an hour," I mutter. "What's the point?"

Tommy stands, "We've gotta have faith, alright? Grab him and bring him back to the car. I'm going to search around for any cameras or prying eyes."

"Alright, good luck."

He gives me an affirming nod, then runs off.

I bend over, scooping Raphael up with both arms. Blood spills from his gut and all over my clean hoodie; it could be a good sign if he's still oozing red. I wince but steadily approach the car. I open the back door, placing his body down across the back seat. Another pool of blood spills out and drenches the black leather. I slide the lower part of his mask back over his mouth before shutting the door. My hands and torso are stained.

Who could've done this?

I get into the front seat and turn on the radio, listening to the calm classical music as it exits the speakers and enters my ears. I rest my head against my seat.

A minute or two goes by before Tommy opens the driver-side door and enters, "There were a few cameras, but nobody else in sight. I think we're good to go."

"Got it. Let's get back to the facility."

CHAPTER NINETEEN

We approach the ginormous hotel owned by Vice – well, *was* owned by Vice. Tommy holds the door open for me, and I enter with Raphael lying limp in my arms.

"Is that the boss?" some guy from behind the desk asks. The overhead lights reflect in the shine of his bald head.

Tommy nods, "Yeah, now open the doors, we've gotta get him out of sight."

The man behind the desk tilts his head forward, reaching his hand somewhere low, I assume to press a button that allows the elevator doors across the lobby to open.

"Thanks, Antonio," Tommy says, escorting me to the cart.

"No problem. Keep me updated."

"I will."

Antonio adjusts his blue tie, telling us to have a good evening.

We enter the elevator, and Tommy hits a button labeled with gibberish.

"Conformation code?" a nonchalant female voice inquires from above.

"Blackest night," he replies.

A loud *ding* chimes out, and the doors reunite.

"Amped up security, huh?" I ask, the sudden drop of the cart causing butterflies to take flight in my gut.

"Bingo. After White started hunting down every top dog here at Lazarus, we took drastic measures. This, here, is the last facility left standing; the rest were blown to pieces, and only a few of us survived as you already know." he stops, and his right eye twitches ever so slightly.

"We can't do this without Raphael," I stare down at the body in my arms, "Please, Tommy. . . Please take my place."

"I can't."

"I'm begging you, man. I can't do this."

"I'm sure he'll be okay. . ."

"When will we know for sure?"

"By morning. Since he's used Rebirth so many times, he'll be showing signs within twelve hours if it worked."

"And for our sakes, it *better* work."

The elevator stops, the doors parting signaled by the chime. Two members stand in our way, but they step aside the moment their eyes meet ours.

"Bleach wants to see him," one remarks with his arms folded.

"Radio her. Tell her that we're bringing him to his dorm room."

"Yes, sir."

The other member nods at me as Tommy and I step out into the corridor. They tell us to update them, and then we're on our way. Our shoes plod against the white tile.

"You're already looking better," he says.

"It's only been a day."

"Still. They fed you absolute crap in Salem. I'm surprised you only lost twenty pounds."

I chuckle, "I look like a twig."

"You kidding me? Sure, you aren't exactly at your prime like you were during Fight-Night, but you definitely don't look like a twig, and with the diet and workout plan you're doing, you'll be back to your peak in no time." He opens a door for me, allowing me to enter the gymnasium. "It's what the Saints do. Have you ever seen a soldier who wasn't jacked?"

"I guess you're right," I readjust Raphael's body so that I don't drop him. "So, *when* he wakes up from his dirt nap, what's next? What's our plan? The God Code will go off soon, and unless we find the thing, everyone will die."

"That's not up for me to decide," he replies. "It's you and him."

"But what if he doesn't make it? Tommy, I can't do this by myself."

"I know, I know. Let me think. I'll talk to Bleach tonight, see what she thinks and all that. If he doesn't come back, then we'll help you. You aren't alone, you know?"

He escorts me to a set of doors before pulling one of them open, allowing me to enter through it. Metal doors adorn each side of the hallway, each with a name stenciled into them. We approach a door that I presume is Raphael's. Tommy turns the knob and pushes it open, and I step in, treading over to the bed before lying Raphael on the mattress.

Bleach enters in from behind us, "How bad is he? What're his injuries?"

I side-step as Tommy hits the lights, permitting her to see the damage that has been done to our leader. Holes litter his clothes. The Kevlar beneath his hoodie is shredded. His jeans are soaked in blood.

"What do you think happened to him?" she asks, examining the corpse with wide eyes.

Tommy shrugs, "No idea. I was talking to Feline when my device went off. Raphael's voice was faint, and he told me his location before saying that he was about to die. That's all he said before the line went dead, and then I destroyed the phone."

"Why'd you destroy it?" I ask.

"We use burner phones to get in touch when our radios are

out of range; we only get to use them once before having to ruin them – too easy to track."

Bleach twiddles her thumbs, "Jason, we need to discuss what needs to happen if he doesn't come back. You're his heir, you're the next in line."

I shake my head, "Please, not now. I don't wanna have to think about it. He should've never made me his successor, it was stupid of him."

She shifts uncomfortably, "Doesn't blot out the fact that he still chose you. You need to have a plan. You have to be prepared."

I open the door and step out. Before continuing down the hall, I look back at the two of them, "Grab me if anything happens."

The door shuts, and I leave them. The silence doesn't get a chance to bother me before the doors at the end of the corridor open. Chloe steps in, a half-smile making an appearance on her face. She gives me a little hug before asking me if Raphael will be okay. Her blonde hair is covering a part of her face.

"I don't know. The situation isn't looking too good."

"What do you mean?"

"Rebirth doesn't work on a host that's been dead for over an hour. He was dead for over an hour and a half."

She stares intensely into my eyes, "What are we going to do if he doesn't wake up?"

"I don't know. Everyone's been asking me that, and honestly, I don't know. Please, can we just not talk about it?"

She compresses her lips and raises an eyebrow, "Yeah, my bad," she grabs me by the arm and begins dragging me along. "Here, what you need is some sleep."

"No, I'm fine."

"It's midnight, and tomorrow is going to be a big day for you."

"Wait, I still need to go hit the weight room."

"Sleep is better."

"Well, yeah, but—"

"Just come on."

She leads me to my dorm door, pushing it open before ushering me inside. After flipping on the lights, I take a deep breath, shedding my bloody hoodie and tossing it across the room. It soaked through and stained my undershirt, so I take that off as well. I walk over to my dresser and pull out black athletic wear.

Chloe heads over to my bed and sits down, "You need to decompress; you have all this built up anxiety and worry inside you. . . kinda emo."

"And how do you know that?" I ask, stepping over to my bed and taking a seat next to her.

"You've been my best friend for how long?"

"Oh, so I'm just your best friend now, huh?"

She rolls her eyes, punching me in the shoulder, "Shut up. You know what I mean."

I let out a slight chuckle, kicking off my shoes, "Yeah. Yeah, I know what you mean."

It goes silent for a moment, and out of the corner of my eye, I see someone standing by the door. Simon.

He winks at me with a stupid grin on his face, and his clothes are too tight, as always.

"What?" Chloe asks, an eyebrow raised. "What's wrong?"

I turn to her, my heart pounding. I try to say something, but smile instead.

Even after being dead, you still find a way to kill the mood.

Chloe places a hand on my thigh, "You're freaking me out."

"What happened to Simon?"

"What? Why are you asking me tha—"

"His body was in the back of the van when we crashed ...," I pause, a lump forming in my throat. "I just want some closure"

She chews her bottom lip, "I can't."

"Why? Chloe, I need this."

"But—"

"Please?"

Her eyes begin to swirl red, and blood trails down her cheeks, "Why do you need to know?"

"He's my best friend."

She forces out an unsteady breath, "You went flying through that windshield. That's all I saw before blacking out, but when I woke up, I was outside of the van – if you could even call it that anymore – and had my hands cuffed behind my back. Saints were everywhere, and I thought you were dead. You were sprawled out across the street, your legs bent backwards, a fifteen-foot trail of blood staining the road from where you slid. Raphael was pushed up against a patrol car by a few Saints; they were pounding him, beating his face in," she pauses, her bottom lip quivering. "Simon, though. . . Simon was lying next to me, his throat still slit open, his body drained of blood. Two Saints came up and grabbed him before tossing him into the back of a black van with those red and blue lights on top. One of them looked back at me and saw me crying. He laughed and told me that he was off to burn Simon at the morgue."

Her words hit me like a train. My stomach is tight, and my chest constricts. There's blood waterfalling down my cheeks, "It's all my fault. If I just would've left Matthew dead all those months ago, then Simon would still be alive."

Chloe carefully scratches my back, "Simon wouldn't want you to blame yourself. He would want you to be happy and to move on."

She's right, which just makes me cry harder. Simon was such a selfless person. He put others before himself. He would do anything to console me or anyone else that was going through a hard time even though his own past was haunting him.

I miss him so much that it hurts.

Chloe wipes her cheeks, "That's all I know, I hope it helps."

I sniffle, "Thanks."

She hugs me, and I wipe my cheeks. She lies down a moment later, and I join her, staring up at the ceiling.

"What if Raphael doesn't come back?" I ask. "I don't want to be responsible for all these people. I don't want to be the one giving out suicide missions. I don't want to be Vice."

"You don't have to be Vice, Jason. You don't have to be anyone but yourself."

"But Lazarus needs someone like Vice; like Raphael. It's like their emotions have been switched off since birth. They don't feel anything."

"When him and I were injected with all those hallucinatory drugs, he begged to die. He kept crying out for his mom, even tried to bite his own tongue off. They had to gag him with cloth so he wouldn't do it. There was even one night where he wouldn't stop bawling, thrashing around in the chair that he was cuffed to. Whatever he was seeing was gnarly."

"But he acts so solid."

"It's his coping mechanism, and plus, he has to be. There's going to be so many other deaths before this is done – on our side and the government's. It's either that, or we just give up and let the God Code take us all out on Christmas Eve."

"But what happens after? What do we do when the fight's over?"

"Start over. Make a better future for everyone."

I smile, "That sounds nice."

She turns to her side, facing me, "It does."

I stare into her eyes, emotion eating away at me, "You aren't going to leave me like he did, are you?"

My words take her aback, "I can't promise anything."

"Just please don't. I can't do this without you."

She stares back at the ceiling, and after a moment, chuckles, "I'm not going anywhere, Jason."

My heart eases, and my mind stops its frenzy of anxiety. She looks back at me and I sink deep into her emerald eyes. Finally, I doze into darkness and a temporary solace.

CHAPTER TWENTY

The sound of my door opening causes my eyes to open. Bleach stands in the entryway.

"What's up?" I greet, rubbing my eyes while sitting up.

Chloe's gone. She must've left after I zonked out.

"He's awake." Bleach utters, her voice overflowing with disbelief. Her jaw is ajar, and sweat dots her forehead.

My eyes go broad, "Are you serious?"

"Yes, but there's a major problem."

"What do you mean?"

"Just follow me."

I stand, slipping my shoes on before stepping out and trailing her down the corridor to Raphael's dorm door. She lightly knocks, and a sudden agonizing scream shoots out, forcing us both to flinch.

"Come in," Tommy shouts.

The inside is dark, absent of all light save the bright lamp illuminating the chair at the back of the room. Tommy is in front of the chair with a scalpel in his hands.

"Is that Pinder?" Raphael asks from the chair.

Tommy nods.

Raphael stands, his clothes still shredded and caked in blood, "Pinder, something went wrong."

He turns around. Vice's mask is still on his face, but the part around his right eye has been cut off, the skin absent underneath. A bloody mess takes the place of flesh.

"What? What is it?" I ask.

"The mask. It's morphed to my face. The nanobots mistook it for a part of my face and knitted it to the flesh," he pauses, blinking his right eye. "I shouldn't be alive. It was over an hour."

My stomach churns, "We can just remove the rest of it, right?"

Tommy shakes his head, "No, but most of it, at least."

"Why only most of it?"

"The area around his left eye is attached so well that if I tried to cut it off, it would blind him."

I stare at Raphael. The mask looks more . . . life-like. It resembles the charred features of a skeleton's face, and its fabric is more metallic and burnt looking than ever.

Bleach opens the door to leave, "I'm gonna step out. Radio me if you need anything."

Tommy nods, and she's gone a second later.

"But he's on Rebirth, won't his sight just come back?" I ask.

Raphael glances over at Tommy, "That's one of the things Rebirth can't do. It can bring back the eye, sure, but not the sight that's supposed to accompany it."

That explains Matthew's eyepatch.

"At least you can get most of it off, right?" I try to comfort him, but his sudden fit of laughter mocks me.

My eyes go wide as he continues to roar with hilarity. He collapses onto the bed, blood streaming out of his right eye. He won't stop; can't stop. I recall that same uncontrollable fit that I had in Vice's office not so long ago.

Tommy looks at me, "Give him a bit of time. Side effects for the enhancement pill are nasty."

I nod, swallowing the memory of noxious hilarity. I turn

around and leave. The sound of Raphael's senseless hysterics burn my eardrums.

※

MY MIND SWIMS IN COUNTLESS THOUGHTS. I TAKE A seat next to Chloe in the cafeteria for lunch. A tray piled high with fish and rice somehow made it into my hands. She and I had been lifting weights in another sector to pass the time. I'm not allowed to eat until eleven, but it must be time.

"It could be worse," she says, taking a sip out of her water. "He could've stayed dead."

"Yeah, I'm just happy he's up and at it," I remark while scooping up a spoonful of food. "Oh, I forgot to ask, how'd you sleep?"

"Great. I went back to my room after you started snoring. It's way comfier and quieter."

"Yeah, whatever."

"No, seriously."

I shove the spoon into my mouth when a pair of hands grab my shoulders from behind.

I flinch, and Exodus laughs, "Gotcha!"

I quickly swallow before saying, "Nice of you to finally join us."

He takes a seat next to me, "Had to get back to my pretty self."

His face is littered with scars and he wears a pair of black shades. He looks good in the Lazarus uniform.

"Why didn't you just take a dose of Rebirth?" I ask.

He sighs, "You're like the eighth person to ask me that."

"And what did you tell them?"

"I have a bit of a phobia when it comes to having little robots swimming around inside my body, and blood coming out of my eyes, make sense?"

Chloe chimes in, "How are you even moving, then? Jason says

you were shot in the chest. No way you could be up and at it after just only three days."

He sighs, "They forced me on it. The bullet hit a vital area, and I was going to die. So, yes, I'm on Rebirth – didn't cure my albinism, though."

"So what? Everyone here is pale, so you should feel right at home," I say.

"It's more than just that."

"You'll live, Blaine."

The doors to the cafeteria open, and the three of us watch Tommy and Bleach enter. They park themselves in front of the crowd of members.

"Listen up," Tommy starts with his arms folded. "Raphael has requested that we pick some of you to go out on a mission for him. When we call your name, come up here."

All the members nod.

"Sam Walker," Bleach begins.

A member with faded dark skin, buzzed hair, and a defiant expression on his face stands from his seat and approaches the two of them.

"Kennedy Allard," Tommy calls.

Kennedy leaves his table, stopping at Sam's side.

"Cass Adams," Bleach volleys.

A girl with long brown hair and hazel eyes makes her way over to Kennedy and Sam.

"Ross Parker," Tommy says.

A member with red hair, brown eyes, and an alluring smile on his face makes his way over to the others.

"And finally," Bleach looks over at our table. "Jason Pinder, Chloe Frye, and Blaine West."

The three of us exchange looks. We get up and head over to join the selected members.

"Come with us," Tommy demands, turning on his heels, opening the doors, and stepping out along with Bleach.

The bright fluorescent lights from above force me to squint. They lead us to an area that's foreign to me. Tommy opens a door, motioning for us to enter.

The room is large. Countless weapons are mounted to the walls; combat knives, sniper and assault rifles, handguns, grenades, syringes, tools, etc.

Bleach turns to us, "Tonight," she says, her eyes meeting mine. "you seven will blow up a hospital."

CHAPTER TWENTY-ONE

I pound my fist against Raphael's door.

"Yeah, go for it," he agrees from inside.

Raphael sits behind a desk that wasn't there just a few hours ago. On it lies a bunch of papers, a handgun, and a few photographs.

He looks up at me. Most of the mask has been cut off, but his left eye is obscured by the metallic material, matching the left side of his jaw.

"A hospital?" I ask. "You want us to go blow up a hospital, and you didn't talk to me about it?"

He nods, grabbing one of the photographs off his desk and handing it to me, "It's a military hospital – hasn't even been opened yet. Nobody's inside."

Upon inspecting the picture in my hand, I raise an eyebrow, "Why are we destroying it, then?"

"We need to slow the Saints down. This hospital has been in the works for over two years, and Mills wants it to be the most sophisticated, state of the art facility ever established. Blowing it up equals pissing in the President's breakfast. . . Plus, we believe that a stolen stash of Rebirth is being stored there, and we want that out of their hands."

"You're right."

"Am I ever wrong?"

"Fair point."

"Look, there's another problem we need to discuss," Raphael's cocky grin fades from his face.

"What is it?"

He leans back in his chair, taking a deep breath, "Those three people who know where the God Code is all have bombs planted inside their skulls in case they talk. Hidden mics are inside all their clothes, and somebody is always watching them."

"What do you mean?"

"I found Murdock in New York – it wasn't hard to track him. He was out taking an evening stroll. Anyway, I abducted him, tortured him, but he wasn't breaking. I knocked him out, and when he woke up, he was inside an old sedan placed in between the two solid walls of a car crusher. He finally started to sing like a bird, but right as he was getting to the important details, his entire head exploded."

"Then what?"

"Mills' voice boomed through a microphone planted inside Murdock's suit coat. He told me that he's always watching, and that's when I was lit up by a sniper. Two Reapers ambushed me, and I took two bullets to the shoulder and ribcage. I was stabbed, shot, beaten, but I got the upper hand and took them out. I had to crawl out of the recycling plant, and I didn't stop until I made it to some park. That's when I called Tommy, but that's all I can remember before dying."

I cross my arms, my mind at work, "What did you get out of Murdock before he was killed?"

"That Mills has the remote that can activate it."

"That really doesn't help us."

"I know, and that's not good considering the fact that the two other men who know where it is are also being watched and have bombs planted inside their heads."

"Could a small EMP disable the bombs?"

"No."

"How do you know?"

"I've seen this before. The bombs Mills has placed inside people's heads have a special outer shell that's resistant to any of that crap. You need a special serum that can eat away at the shell and disable the explosive."

"Do we have any of that?"

"Of course, but we'd be killed before we could even get that close. I don't know why the sniper took so long to take his shot at me. Plus, after what happened to Murdock, I'm sure Mills has the other two in hiding."

I glance at a metallic mask similar to Vice's on the table. It's amped though, and it seems to have some type of armor-like material coating it.

"What is that?" I ask, pointing at the new mask.

He smirks, looking over at the object, "It's a little project I'm working on. It's a mask that will hide your identity; it also has Kevlar padding underneath, and the metal I used is bullet resistant."

"Is it for you?"

"I want everyone to have one. This is just a little prototype. But anyway, is your mind all clear? Are you ready for tonight?"

I tilt my head in reply, "Yeah. I'm gonna go hit the showers and prepare. I'll make sure to stop by before my group and I leave."

"Alright, see you in a bit."

I turn to leave, but stop short from the door, "Raph?"

"Yeah?"

"Why am I still your heir? Why not Tommy?"

"Do you remember the first night you became an official member?"

My mind forces unnecessary images into itself, "How could I forget?"

"What you did reminded me of something I would do, and great minds think alike."

"Tommy has more experience."

"Sure, but he doesn't have the same mindset that you and I both share."

My shoulders slump, "But what happens if you bite the dust and don't come back? You and I both know that I'm not ready to be the leader."

"You're right, you aren't ready, but neither was I."

Without another word, I leave his office.

CHAPTER TWENTY-TWO

Mist escapes from my mouth with each breath, and the moon overhead illuminates the seven of us. We stand ready on a rooftop directly across from the hospital. It's late, and the streets below are empty except for the occasional patrol car that passes through.

The watch on Exodus' wrist goes off, and he looks at me, "It's go time."

I cast my gaze on Cass, "Drop your bag," I turn to the others. "Each of you need to grab an E-772. Don't forget that the trigger also controls your speed."

Everyone takes turns grabbing a grapple gun, and after I get mine, I take a step back.

"Do you have the charges?" Chloe asks Ross.

"Yep, they're in my bag," he replies.

I turn to Exodus, "And you have the detonator?"

He nods. his snow-white hair grazing his shades.

Small pops come from Kennedy as he loosens up his neck, "And we're still sticking to the plan Tommy and Bleach briefed us with?"

"Yeah," I reply, stepping up on the cement barrier of the roof.

"Now come on. We have ten minutes before we have to be out of there."

"What if we run into any Saints?" Sam asks, stepping up by my side.

"Take them out quietly. We don't want tonight to be a bloodbath."

"Got it."

Everyone steps up to the barrier, and I initiate the next step by aiming my grapple gun up at the hospital's roof and firing. It takes a moment, but the hook connects, and I leap off the building, picking up immense speed before putting pressure on the trigger to slow me down.

Unwanted memories of the night I went out for revenge plays through my mind, and I cringe thinking of how things would be different if I would've left Matthew dead.

I'm sorry, Simon.

The seven of us reach the rooftop one after another. Cass is last.

"You four have the first five floors," I order Exodus, Sam, Ross and Kennedy. I glance over at Chloe and Cass, "And we have the last four."

They nod, and Ross drops his backpack before reaching in and pulling out some of the charges. We each get three, and after that, the four assigned to the beginning levels of the hospital head toward the elevator doors. Exodus hits the call button, and a few moments later, the doors slide open.

"Looks like we're taking the stairs," Chloe pulls a cold steel door open.

Cass and I follow Chloe, and we clamber down two sets of metal stairs before the first door on the right appears. The sound of our steps on the metal echo through the stairwell.

Cass stops, telling us that she'll take the ninth and eighth floor. We agree, and she disappears.

"I'll take the seventh floor," Chloe tells me as we climb down some more stairs.

"Alright, guess that leaves me with the sixth. You have your radio on you, right?"

"Right."

We stop at another door. Chloe opens it.

"Good luck," I say, and she winks at me.

"You too."

All by myself, I head down another flight of stairs. The three charges in my backpack slow me down a bit. When I open the fifth-floor door, I notice that all light is absent, so I have to feel around the walls until I find a switch.

Bingo.

The floor lights up, and I take a look around. I'm in a large lobby-like area with a long desk off to my side where I assume a receptionist will work. I look at the words stenciled into the desk's brown oak, it taking a moment for my mind to un-jumble the words.

Eventually, I'm able to make out *Intensive Care*.

I take off my backpack and set it down on the desk, unzipping it and pulling out a hefty explosive. I glance around the lobby, scoping out the best place to set it.

I approach a window to my far left, placing a single charge beneath it. I then pull another charge from my backpack and head over to large column placed dead center of the lobby, planting the explosive against its plastered surface.

For my last charge, I'm a bit more selective with my placement. I head down a long corridor with rooms on each side, and turn right down another hall. At the end of it, there's a pair of double doors with a sign on them that reads something in bold red letters. When I enter, I am surprised to be greeted by a large amount of oxygen canisters. I also see vials of liquid placed everywhere that are labeled with the same bold red letters that were placed over the doors.

I walk up to one of the oxygen canisters, placing the charge over it before leaving the room. I don't get too far before my radio goes off.

"I'm done with my floors," Kennedy states.

"Me too," Sam follows.

"And me," Ross says.

Both girls also say that they're done.

I wait a moment. I put my radio up to my mouth and hold a button down, "What about you, Exodus? Is your floor done?"

No reply.

"Exodus?" I call out again. "You there, man?"

Another moment goes by without a reply, and before I have the chance to press the button again, a voice pours through.

"Guys, we've gotta problem," Exodus whispers.

"What is it?" Chloe asks.

"We've got company. Eight patrol cars just pulled up. I'm heading to the rooftop now."

I attempt to press the panic down in my gut, "Everyone get back up to the roof *now.*"

They all voice in their affirmatives. I rush out the door and sprint back into the stairwell, climbing the stairs. My steps echo through the hollow stairwell.

The cool Autumn air hits me in the face as I step out onto the roof. My eyes meet Chloe first, relief filling my chest. Cass is by her side.

"Where are the rest?" I ask them, but they shrug.

I look over to the edge of the structure. The flashing blue and red lights bounce off the surrounding buildings. Thunder cracks overhead, and raindrops start to fall.

I grab my radio and force the button down, "Where are you guys? We've gotta split."

I wait a moment.

"We're almost there. In the elevator now."

I clip my radio back onto my jeans, looking over the city. More and more patrol cars speed down the street and park in front of the hospital. A unit of Saints spill out of a large van with canines strapped to leashes. They howl, bark, and sneer, begging to be released.

Memories of Nacht-Fest enter my mind, and I let a little smile escape.

It was all so simple back then.

The chime of the elevator doors opening disrupts my thoughts. Exodus, Ross, Sam, and Kennedy step out of the metal box and into the night.

The rain falls harder, and another crack of thunder bursts throughout the sky.

I motion them to me, and I reach into my backpack and pull out my grapple gun. They do the same, and after confirming once more that all the charges were planted, I turn and fire my line at the towering building opposite to us. The hook hits its mark, and I leap from the roof. The rain and wind hit my face as I fly through the air.

I briefly look down to watch a sea of Saints storm the hospital. The howls from the canines ricochet inside my ears. I fly toward my destination. My right-hand grabs hold of the building's ledge when I hit the end of my steel line.

I pull myself up, getting to my feet.

The others make it one by one. After the last member touches the rooftop, I signal Exodus, "Blow it."

He reaches into his back pocket, pulling out the detonator, "Sweet."

He presses his thumb down on the only button the device has.

I face the hospital and watch it burst into a fireball. Debris flies everywhere, and I lunge out of the way as chunks of the building soar toward us. They hit the roof, taking out a large exhaust vent and missing Ross by just a few inches.

I carefully head over to the edge, and look down. I don't see anything but smoke and dust. I take a step back, until my eyes find Chloe.

"How did they find us?" I ask. "And are you okay?"

She shrugs, "Security cameras? Or maybe a patrol saw us enter. And yes, I'm okay, you?"

"Yeah, I'm good," I turn to the others. "Let's head back to the facility before backup arrives."

We move to the other side of the roof, and aim our grapple guns toward another building. We leap off, leaving behind the carnage.

CHAPTER TWENTY-THREE

M aking it back to the facility is difficult, but we eventually find ourselves outside of the double doors that lead into the hotel. The inside is extravagant; high ceilings adorned with built in lights, couches in the lobby that are soft to the touch, carpets with abstract-like designs, and a plate of cookies out on a cherry oak desk.

The man behind the desk, Antonio, sees us, and hits a button that remotely unlocks the doors. I push one of them open, the rest following in behind me.

"How'd the mission go?" he asks me.

"Great. The hospital's gone, and so are about thirty Saints."

"I thought there weren't supposed to be any casualties?"

"Yeah, well play stupid games, win stupid prizes. A bunch of patrols stormed the hotel trying to get to us, but we escaped and blew it before they even knew what was going on."

Antonio nods, pressing another button that wirelessly opens the elevator doors, "I see. Alright, well go check in with the boss. He's anxious to hear how it went."

"Got it," the seven of us head to the elevator. "Have a good night, man."

"You too, sir."

I press the lowest button on the control panel, and a casual female voice asks for the confirmation code, to which I reply, "Blackest night."

The doors shut, and the elevator lowers.

"Good job, everyone," I express while leaning against the back wall of the cart.

Chloe holds my hand, and my heart stutters, "Yeah, you all did great."

There's a moment of silence, smooth jazz coming from overhead, soothing to my ears.

"So," Kennedy starts, pulling the bandana from his face and stuffing it into his back pocket, "how do you feel about being the new heir? Is it stressful?"

Cass rolls her eyes, "What kind of question is that? Of course, it's stressful, especially with everything that's been happening lately."

He sighs, "Well, maybe he doesn't feel the same way you do, have you ever thought about that?"

"Whatever, dude."

I open my mouth to say something, but Simon appears in front of me. His grey eyes sweep me, and I flinch back, crashing my head against the wall.

"A hospital, huh?" he says with a grin on his face.

My heart speeds up, hammering inside my chest.

Chloe looks over at me, "What's wrong?"

Kennedy raises an eyebrow, "Yeah, you okay, boss?"

Simon turns his back to me, "You look thirstier than a teenage girl. Might want to go get some water after this, alright?" he glances at my shoes, "Dehydration isn't a joke."

I slap the side of my head, and he disappears, leaving behind an elevator full of concerned stares.

"It's nothing," I attempt to regain my posture. "Just tired." The lift stops, and the doors slide open with a *ding*. I quickly step out.

RAPHAEL SITS BEHIND HIS DESK, LEANING BACK IN HIS chair with his feet propped up on the wooden surface while Chloe voices her concerns.

"The hospital job was reckless," she says, sweeping a stray strand of blonde hair out of her eyes. "We need to be focusing more on the God Code."

He lowers his feet, "I know, Frye, but Vincent Murdock was the only lead we had, and now he's dead, so what do you propose?"

I shift, "What about that remote you were telling me about? If it could activate it, couldn't it hypothetically deactivate it, too? If we get it, we can shut it down, couldn't we?"

"Yes, probably, but do you realize what would have to be done in order for that to happen?"

Exodus is casually leaning against the wall. His dark shades cover his pale blue eyes, "A lot."

A sudden knock at the door interrupts our conversation.

Raphael looks past me, "Who is it?"

"Lynch. I have bad news."

"Come in, then."

The door hinges swivel back, and in walks the man who helped me win Fight-Night. He sees me, and a wide grin appears on his face. He doesn't look much different. His head is shaved, and his eyes are dark. "Jason?"

"It's been so long."

He clasps my hand, pulling me in and patting me on the back, "I didn't know you were here, kid. I thought you died back in Salem."

"Well, I wouldn't be alive if it weren't for all the training you gave me," I turn to Raphael. "How come I didn't know Lynch was here? I haven't seen him once."

"That's because he's been in the infirmary."

Lynch chimes in, "That's what I came to talk to you about. In private."

Raphael looks over at Chloe and Exodus, "Go down to the barracks for a debriefing."

The two of them nod, and they leave after saying bye. I watch Chloe as she heads out, and when our eyes meet, she smiles.

I glance over at Raphael, "What about me? You need me to go?"

"You're my heir. You get to stay."

Lynch's mouth parts. He holds a look of pride in his eyes, "You're the new heir?"

I nod, "Only because he thought no one else was alive."

He snorts, "So? I told you that you had potential back in our training days. Good job, kid."

Raphael moves us along, "What's the bad news?"

Lynch regroups himself, folding his arms, "Our Rebirth supply is running dry – two or three more syringes, that's it. The rest has either been destroyed, or taken by the government."

Raphael's one visible eye widens, "Wait, seriously? Why haven't I been told about this sooner?"

"I don't know; Tommy is the one who sent me here to tell you."

Raphael grits his teeth, "But how? I don't understand how we're running dry. This is the only facility that Mills doesn't know about. Hell, I didn't even know about it until just the other day. Vice wanted this to be the facility Lazarus used for their last stand – it's supposed to have more than enough of everything, and that includes Rebirth."

Lynch shakes his head, "I don't know what to tell you, sir."

It grows silent; the only sound is the clock ticking up on the wall.

"We'll have to make more," Raphael eventually says. "Vice knew the person who made the serum; he knew how to make it."

I look at him, "Do you have the instructions?"

Lynch abruptly stumbles backward, clutching his face with both hands.

"Lynch?" his name leaves my mouth as he begins screaming simultaneously.

Raphael stands, "What's wrong? Lynch—"

"*It's the numbers!*" he screams, his back slamming against the door. "*They're playing in my head!*"

"Good evening, Cyrus Kruger," the voice of our president booms through an unknown device located somewhere on my old instructor. "Kill Raphael Ramirez and Jason Pinder without mercy."

My eyes widen as Lynch pulls a handgun out of his back pocket and aims it at Raphael.

I lunge forward and tackle Lynch to the floor. He manages to pull the trigger when we both hit the ground, the bullet flies, and Raphael yelps as I pin Lynch's wrists to the floor.

He breaks loose and slams the pistol into the side of my face. I retaliate by crushing his nose with my palm, forcing blood to stream out of his nostrils.

I swear as he knocks me off, turning the tables and pinning me to the floor with one hand, the other holding the gun to my temple.

Three gunshots go off, and brain matter sprays from Lynch's skull. He buckles off of me, and I scramble to my feet, looking at Raphael who's holding the smoking end of a pistol in his right hand. He uses his left to hold the bleeding wound in his shoulder.

Insane laughter bursts from the unknown device attached to Lynch's motionless body, "How did you two gentlemen like my little surprise? You see, back when I had my men storm Vice's facility, we found some very intriguing technology – but by far Rewired is the most intriguing out of them all. Yes, resurrection serums are quite fascinating, but to be able to completely control a host with just the sound of my voice? Oh, it's phenomenal!"

Raphael grits his teeth, "You filthy capullo. . ."

More laughter erupts from the device, "Losing your temper there, Mr. Ramirez? White told me that you never lost your temper, and how you had to feel superior to everyone else. Do you feel superior now, boy?"

"How did you find Lynch?" I ask, spit flying from my mouth. "How did you find us?"

"Oh, Jason. . . you've always been such a pathetic angry kid, haven't you? My military stormed every facility that Lazarus had. Well, at least I thought they did, but I guess you had one last trick up your sleeve. Anyway, Mr. Kruger was a feisty one, oh yes, but the bigger they are, the harder they fall," he pauses to clear his throat. "He was shot and bleeding out, but Matthew had a better idea rather than finishing him off with a simple bullet to the head; he took him to my scientists, along with all the brilliant technology he found. While your friend was unconscious and dying, we put him through Rewired, made him my puppet," he laughs. "We threw him out onto the streets after that, and it wasn't long before he woke up and contacted you traitors. . . wanna know the best part about this all?"

Raphael and I don't reply.

"The chip we planted inside his head has a tracker."

Lynch's head explodes, painting the room red. More laughter echoes inside the room.

"Just in case you had thoughts of bringing him back from the dead," Mills wheezes, coughing and laughing like an absolute madman.

The radio attached to Raphael's waist begins screaming, "Sir! Sir, armed Saints are storming into the hotel, they've found us! We're going to—"

Gunshots interpose, leaving a staticky silence.

CHAPTER TWENTY-FOUR

"Where are the others?" Raphael asks as we rush down the hallway.

"I don't know," I reply, running faster. "But we have time. The Saints don't know the code to access the facility, and since Antonio's dead, they won't be able to get it."

He nods, the two of us stopping in front of the double doors. He opens one and enters, and I follow behind. We're in the gymnasium, but get stopped at the sight of Tommy, Bleach, Chloe, and Exodus standing just feet away, panting.

"Did you hear about the breach?" Bleach asks.

"Yes, now we need to think, and quick. Where are the other members?" Raphael asks back.

Tommy points over to another pair of doors, "They're all in their rooms winding down for the night, what happened to Lynch? Where is he? I sent him down to tell you about Rebirth."

I shake my head, "He's dead."

Chloe's eyes widen, "Dead? How?"

Raphael takes a deep breath, "He was put through Rewired. He led the Saints right to us, and we had to kill him since he was trying to take us out."

Bleach chambers a round into her gun, "Okay, so what now? What do we do?"

"You, Jason, Chloe, and Exodus are going to go help the members guarding the elevator. Tell them that they need to dismantle it and keep it from functioning," he pauses, gazing over at Tommy. "You and I are going to go arm the other members and get them ready for the fight."

We all nod. Raphael and Tommy rush to the dormitory, and Bleach, Chloe, Exodus, and I sprint to the doors that'll take us to the sector with the elevator. The two members are already working on shutting it down as we approach them. Once they see us, they tell us that there's a problem with the scanner, and how they won't be able to take it off without the proper tools.

Bleach looks back at me, "Go find Raphael. He always carries a multitool on him."

I do as I'm told, but the sudden sound of the elevator motioning up causes me to pause, "They just called it. They bypassed the code."

The two members stand staring down at their handguns. One of them glances at Bleach, "This won't be enough. We need shotguns, rifles, explosives."

She steps forward, "I know, I know. Look, they'll only be able to fit eight or so of them in the cart at a time. We can fight them off while Raphael and Tommy are getting the others ready," she turns to Chloe and Exodus. "Go tell everyone that they bypassed the code. Get geared up yourselves, and be quick."

The two of them nod before spinning around.

I pull my handgun out of my back pocket and switch off the safety, taking a deep breath, "We won't be able to hold them off forever. Maybe one or two patrols at least, but there's only four of us."

One of the members looks back. He's young, maybe around my age, "Sir, you and Bleach need to go open two of the classroom doors; they're heavy and will help protect you."

I make my way to one of the classroom doors and pull it open.

"I'll take that one," Bleach says, softly pushing me out of the way.

"Why?" I ask.

"You're the heir. These doors won't hold up, and I'm not going to let you get killed."

"Marcy," my stomach knots up. "None of us are dying tonight, okay?"

I know that's a lie.

"Hopefully not," her face is pale, and her eyes swirl with anxiety. "Hurry and get behind another door."

I step back a few feet, pulling open another door and using it as a shield.

One of the members in front of the elevator glances at us, "It's coming back down. Get ready. The two of us are going to catch them off guard."

Bleach and I nod, and no more than ten seconds later, the chiming *ding* of the elevator booms out. The doors slide open, and my eyes go abnormally wide as two Saints step out. They have riot shields in their hands, metal helmets over the heads, and their entire bodies are covered in heavy battle armor.

The two members turn to retreat, but the six Saints behind the two juggernauts open fire, shredding the two men with bullets. They collapse and skid across the floor. Blood gushes onto the white marble floor. The Saints continue to fill the corpses with bullets, making today's dinner rush up my throat.

I quickly swallow.

Marcy peeks her gun over the door and fires, but the riot shields absorb the blast.

I peek over and aim at the first Juggernaut's foot, squeezing the trigger and sending a bullet into his boot. He screams, but that doesn't stop him from marching forward with his companion.

The six Saints exit the elevator, and I flinch as they open fire.

Bleach's door is ripped apart, bullets tearing through the wood and spattering her with holes.

I scream her name, rushing out from behind my door and tackling her, forcing her into the adjoining classroom. We hit the floor, and the door shuts behind me. I quickly turn and lock it, knowing it won't do anything but delay the inevitable.

Bleach's clothes are tattered, and blood begins pooling around her.

"Marcy!" I yell, rushing to her side. "Marcy, you're going to be okay."

Her eyes are wide, and a trickle of blood spills from the corner of her lips. She coughs, and my face gets splattered.

"Marcy, please!" I cry out. My heart is pounding, and the rosy-red tears trickle down my cheeks.

She was the first person I saw after waking up from my first death all those months ago. She answered my questions, had my back, and now she's lying in a pool of her own blood, convulsing.

She lets out one last ragged breath, then. . . she's gone, her stare blank and foggy.

The door is kicked in behind me, and I prepare myself to meet the same fate.

"Hands in the air!" one of the soldiers blurt.

I don't know how to react. I can't even move. I can't think.

A boot flies into my face, and I collapse to my side. A Saint rips the gun out of my hand, tosses it across the room, and turns me to my back, placing me in handcuffs.

What's going on?

After he's done, he unclips his radio from his vest and holds a button down, "We have Pinder, sir."

"Good," Matthew's voice pours through. "Keep him and the few other targets alive. Another patrol is on their way down along with a few Reapers. Kill anyone that isn't needed breathing."

"Yes, sir. What should we do with Pinder while we storm the rest of the facility?"

"Inject him. I don't want him starting any more trouble."

"Yes, sir."

I flinch as a needle is shoved into the side of my neck and a cool liquid fills my body. I struggle to stay awake, but I can't fight against whatever's in me. The last thing I see before blacking out is Bleach's wide eyes.

CHAPTER TWENTY-FIVE

My eyes shoot open. The area is dark and cool. It takes my mind a few moments to find its way through the haze. I can see that I'm sitting in an armchair across from President Mills. He sits in a matching chair with his hands clasped on his lap. His face lacks any sign of emotion.

A set of glass double doors lead to a balcony on my left. The moonlight is the only thing illuminating the room. My nose throbs.

"Would you like some coffee?" he asks me. The cane he used to kill Vice rests against his knee.

I don't respond. I just stare at him, my gaze narrowed. I'm not handcuffed or restrained in any sort of way, which unnerves me.

"I don't drink coffee," I finally mutter.

"Perhaps some wine?"

"Go to hell, Joseph."

Mills' expression tenses, then relaxes, "You're so. . . brash, Jason."

"Why am I here?"

He places his right hand atop the cane, rubbing the golden

handle with his thumb, "Am I not allowed to converse with a young member of my society?"

I laugh, then stand, gnashing my teeth, "Cut the crap, Mills. Cut the crap before I—"

"Sit down," he orders, his voice tame but ruthless. "Now!"

"I should just kill you," I spit as images of Bleach burn through my skull, shattering my heart.

At first, he laughs, but then his voice grows low and turns into a snarl, "I've been quite generous, Jason. I kept you alive, allowed you to be in my presence without a gun to your head, and with no restraints around your body. Sit down before I regret my decision."

I debate my next move carefully and gradually lower myself into the armchair, "You should know by now that keeping me alive is only going to cause you pain and misery."

"Perhaps you're right. Perhaps I should just put a bullet in you now and be done with this childish rebellion of yours," he pauses, his lips curling into a sinister grin. "But where would the fun in that be?"

"*Fun?*" I practically spit the word. "What about this is *fun?* People continue to die every day; children becoming orphans, women turning into widows – it's a bloodbath."

"And whose fault is that?"

My eyes broaden and my fingers twitch, "*Yours.*"

"There's so much you don't understand, Jason; so much you couldn't even begin to comprehend," he stops, taking a moment to compose himself. "You can't change a thing – you think you can, but that's just one of the many lies you tell yourself. Tell me, how is Lazarus any different than the Saints? You terrorists try so desperately hard to overthrow me due to my ideology, but tell me, how was your pathetic little leader, Vice, any different? You really think he wanted to overthrow me to restore the way this nation used to be? Don't be so juvenile; he wanted to overthrow me so that he could be the one in power. So he could be the one who sat on the throne. Face it, Jason, you're working for a group that goes off the philosophy of a power-hungry lunatic."

"You lie, just as you always do. I'm not – *we're* not anything like you or your bloodthirsty military."

"Don't kid yourself. How many of my men have you killed? Just in the last month. No remorse, no second thoughts, no humanity. I saw the footage of you out on your killing spree; murdered so many good men who did nothing to you."

"*Nothing* to me? Two of your men executed my parents right in front of me before putting a bullet through my neck! The Saints slaughter so many people each day that I'm surprised you still have a population to rule. You know you're the bad guy, so why try and convince me otherwise?"

He cocks his head to the side, "How brainwashed are you? Without me, we wouldn't even be here."

I grit my teeth, "What do you want from me? This little chat of ours is pointless, so cut to the chase. Why am I sitting across from you? Why am I even alive?"

He leans back a bit, crossing one leg over the other, his cane held firmly in his grip, "The answer is simple, really. I want you to work for me."

I sputter with laughter, but it turns into a low growl, "Screw you."

"Right now, I have what remains of Lazarus held captive throughout the Estate – which is where you are at, at the moment. Each one of you has a bomb planted inside your skull, and at any given time, I can press a button that will rupture your brains."

My eyes widen, my heart pumping, "You're lying."

"Hmm, about what? Having your people held captive? Or the bombs?"

"Both, you crazy prick. . ."

He grins wildly, clapping his hands twice. The large oak doors to the room open, and in walks a young woman wearing a maid's uniform. She stops herself in front of Mills before handing him a device.

He nods, and she leaves, shutting the doors behind her.

Mills taps the screen a few times before tossing the phone over to me. I catch it, looking down at the screen.

My jaw drops.

The screen is divided into three sections, each one containing footage of my friends.

Raphael hangs from a chandelier with a blindfold covering his face. Two Reapers pound his torso with metal batons. Exodus is strapped down to a bed and is waterboarded by two other gas mask wearing freaks. And Chloe is forced down against the floor by two Saints. One of them is licking her face.

My body trembles, a mix of emotions stirring through me, "No. . . No, no, no, no."

Mills stands from his chair, "You have until morning to make up your mind. If you say yes, you and your friends will begin working for me; but if you say no, all of you will die in hideous ways. First, I'll make you watch your girlfriend get chopped into little tiny pieces and fed to my dog, then I'll force you to watch the two others get their brains blown out. To finish it all off, I'll have you buried alive, leaving you to suffocate in a dark, cold place," he rises and opens one of the doors. "Choose wisely. Oh, and the bomb in your head is set to go off if you leave the room before morning. Don't be stupid."

He steps out, leaving me in a dark bedroom by myself.

This can't be happening.

I stare down at the screen once more, watching my three partners get tortured in horrendous ways.

Observing Chloe is unbearable. The two Saints beat her, only stopping to lick her face.

I'll kill you both.

I chuck the phone against the wall before grasping my hair

with both hands and tugging. I snarl, eventually letting out a full-fledged scream.

Lazarus has lost. Everyone minus a few are dead, and it's up to me to decide if we go extinct or not. Why is Mills doing this? He plans on killing everyone in two months, so why put us through this? Why have us work for him?

I stand from the chair before flinging it across the room. It sends splinters everywhere as it breaks against the floor. I stand still, and a faint beeping emits from inside my skull.

I'm trapped here, incapable of leaving, my free will gone and burnt to ashes.

My eyes wander to the security camera that stalks me, its blinking green light assuring me that it's on. I flip it off before turning around and eyeing the bed in front of me. The soft quilt that's draped over the mattress is black and red. It entices me to rest.

I step forward but quickly stop myself. My mind screams at me to walk away. He wants me to relax, to be comfortable and to make himself seem like the good guy or the bigger man.

I swivel around, approaching the other armchair that isn't destroyed and sit down.

After a few hours of being still and thinking, my eyes grow heavy, but I refuse to sleep. I refuse to relax because that's just what he wants. I won't familiarize myself with this hellish place.

Another hour passes, then another, and finally, my eyes have had enough, defying my wishes they shut.

CHAPTER TWENTY-SIX

My eyes open to the sound of a door opening. The same maid from last night enters my room. Her eyes are hypnotizing, but her expression is emotionless.

She approaches me with a pressed black suit in her hand along with some other items. She places them on the bed, then turns to me, "Good morning, Mr. Pinder. The President has requested your presence, and requires you to wear something more presentable."

I stand from the chair, my eyes narrowed, "What? Is my clothing not good enough, princess?"

She doesn't reply, so I step over to the bed, pulling my hoodie off and tossing it to the floor before shedding my white undershirt.

The maid stares, and I don't bother to tell her to look away.

After stripping down to my boxers, I grab the white dress shirt off the bed and slip it on, buttoning it up before grabbing the black tie that accompanies it. I stare at it for a moment, eventually looping it around my collar.

"Is something wrong?" the maid asks after a few prolonged moments of nothing, her black bangs partially obscuring her sight.

I glance over at her, feeling my face tighten, "I don't know how to tie a tie."

She doesn't say a word, instead she steps up to me and begins doing what my dad always had to do.

I feel vulnerable, and once she's done, I abruptly turn around and grab the pair of black slacks. I slide them up my legs and button them up. Finally, I grab a dark belt and loop it through.

"You're young," I say, putting on a pair of dress socks. "How old are you?"

"Nineteen," she replies in a soft voice.

"Why are you working for the president?"

"That's none of your concern."

I slip on the black dress shoes, "Fair enough."

After donning the black suit coat and buttoning it up, I turn to leave, but she stops me.

"What's wrong?" I ask, my mind a mess, my thoughts all over the place.

"Your hair," she gets up on her tip toes and runs her hand through my dirty blonde mop, smoothing the loose strands. "It's too messy to be seen by our ruler."

I roll my eyes, and after she's done, the two of us exit the room and head down the long hallway. The walls are white and adorned with art. Chandeliers hang fifteen feet above, and the carpet is cherry red and perfect cushioning for my feet. The soft fabric is enticing to both the eye and the physical touch.

She leads me down countless other hallways before we stop in front of a grand staircase. I take the first step, but she stops me, pulling me back and looking me in the eyes.

"Why do you do what you do?"

I raise an eyebrow, "What?"

"You're the heir to a terrorist organization, and you're what? Seventeen? Eighteen?"

"That's none of your concern."

I turn away and climb up the stairs, not waiting for her. Once we get to the top, she leads me down another two halls before stopping in front of a cherry oak door guarded by two Reapers. Their stoic stares aren't averted by my presence. Their uniforms are pristine, the gas masks they wear are as dark as midnight, and the gripped shotguns are shiny and ready to kill.

I think back to the Reaper who killed Brandon Yancy. He was so cold and merciless.

Much like me now.

Images of all those I've killed flash through my mind, and my heart stops for a beat or two.

"State your business," one of the Reapers commands. His voice is modulated and metallic.

"President Mills has requested this man's presence," my escort replies.

The other Reaper scoffs, his voice sending a chill down my spine, "Man? This boy isn't a man; he's a coward, nothing but a waste of precious space."

"Bite me," I mutter, my stare frigid.

The Reaper reaches out and grabs me by the neck, pulling me in closer, "Oh, I will—"

"Stop it," the maid demands, her voice a mere squeak compared to the guards. "The President has ordered that no one is to touch him."

The Reaper lets me go, and my chest burns with rage. I want to tackle him to the floor, to rip his stupid mask off and to shove the barrel of a gun up against his temple and blow his brains out.

The other guard opens the door, and the two of them step aside, allowing me to enter. The maid doesn't follow me in, and the door is shut behind me.

The room is small yet elaborately decorated. Mills sits behind a desk cluttered in books and papers. He's in a suit, much like my own, and his cane is still held tightly in his grip.

Another Reaper is in the room, standing next to a bookshelf to my right. He holds an assault rifle in his hands, and his finger is on the trigger.

"Good morning, Jason," Mills greets, motioning to the chair in front of his desk. "Come, sit down."

I do as I'm told, not uttering a word.

The room is silent for a few moments, but he eventually speaks.

"How did you sleep?"

I don't reply.

The Reaper steps forward, towering over me, "Speak when spoken to."

I glance over at him before bringing my attention back to Mills, "What happens if I haven't made up my mind?"

"Then all those events I told you about last night will come to pass," he pauses with an intrigued look on his face. "But something tells me that you have made up your mind, even if you haven't realized it, yet."

I lean back in the chair, "Why are you doing this? You already plan on killing everyone on December 24th, so why go through all this trouble to have me and what remains of Lazarus to work for you?"

He chuckles, groping his cane's handle, "That information is something I won't discuss with you. Now listen, and listen carefully. I'm giving you a minute to tell me your answer, and if you don't, I'll snap my fingers and your girlfriend will be chopped up and fed to my pooch."

The Reaper tosses a device onto my lap, and I look down at the footage of Chloe tied down to a bed with a man at her side hovering an axe over her neck.

My throat closes, my eyes widen, and sweat dots my forehead, "She didn't do anything to you."

He puts a finger up to his lips, "*Shhh!* Stay quiet and think. Think hard, but quick."

Last night, I didn't think about my decision. I wouldn't allow myself to bend to his will, but now here I am, sitting in a chair watching Chloe strapped to a bed with a sharp weapon over her throat.

If I say no, she and the others will die; but if I say yes, we'll be forced to be Mills' slaves until he finds another use for us. There's no winning here, and I'm running out of time.

"Thirty seconds, Jason," he informs me.

I stare at the screen. Tears stream down her face, and there's blood dripping from her bottom lip.

Think! Think, think, think! I'm going to die, she's going to die, we're all going to die if I don't think!

My fingers curl into fists, my knuckles turning white.

"Twenty seconds."

My eyes shoot all across the room, my mind all over the place.

I can't think.

Everything inside my head is fried; hot to the touch.

"Ten seconds."

Submit to him. Be loyal and sufficient, and when the time is right, kill him and escape.

"Five seconds."

But what about the God Code? Time is running out.

"Jason," Mills starts, staring at me with an unreadable look on his face. "Your time is up."

"I—" the words don't come willingly, so I force them to. "I'm yours. I belong to you. . . sir."

He grins, "I'm glad to see that you've come to your senses," he stands, stepping out from behind his desk and stopping at my side. "Now you and your friends will be sent down to my torture chamber for two weeks."

My eyes widen, my breath comes out short and unsteady, "What? Why?"

He laughs, "Do you really think I would trust an assassin who wants my head to work for me without being broken down and defeated first?" He grabs my face with one hand. "I'm not a fool, Jason."

The stock of a gun rams into my face, and my eyes roll into the back of my head, leaving me to drown in a murky black ocean of darkness. All I hear is an unbearable ringing in my ears accompanied by a timely beeping.

CHAPTER TWENTY-SEVEN

Fingernails are ripped off with pliers, I'm beaten with all manner of blunt weapons, and I am cuffed to a cold metal chair inside a dark, freezing room with a single TV mounted to the wall that's used to show me security footage of my parents' execution. They force me to watch this all day, every day. Hooks are used to keep my eyelids open, eyedrops are used to keep my irises from shriveling up, and I'm not allowed to sleep.

For days on end, I'm injected with drugs that bring my nightmares to life, forcing me to vividly hallucinate about all of the people I've killed. They stand in front of me, naked and pale, blood staining their walking corpses. All they do is sob, howl, and gnash their teeth, asking me why I took their lives away.

The guilt eats me alive as the days pass. The dead haunt me. Regret fills my chest, and even though the people I've killed were my enemies, it doesn't stop me from begging them to forgive me.

"*I'm sorry!*" I scream, bloody tears bursting from my eyes. "*Please, please I'm sorry!*"

Eventually, the torture numbs me, leaving me absent of all emotion. I see the dead constantly. I physically can't shut my eyes, but even if I could, I doubt that it would stop their visages from clouding my vision. I'm exhausted, but a Reaper comes in every few hours and injects me with something that leaves me unable to go unconscious

I puke out what little is in my stomach, leaving my mouth with the bitter taste of stomach acid.

The door to my room opens. The TV's bright light illuminates a Reaper as he approaches me. He throws a hand into my face, and my nose snaps out of place, red gushing from my nostrils.

"You're nothing," he mutters, throwing another punch. "You're all alone."

I spit a mouthful of blood out onto the floor, splattering the cement.

I'm only wearing my boxers, and I have been sitting in my own filth for over a week. The cold is reminiscent of Salem's chill.

The Reaper pulls a polaroid picture out of his back pocket and shows it to me.

It's a picture of Chloe, lying on the floor, unconscience.

He tosses it to the ground before bending over and picking up a jug of water that he and the others have done unspeakable things to before forcing me to drink some, pouring the rest over my frozen body.

"I promise you—" I utter through chattering teeth. I'm shivering uncontrollably.

"You promise me what?" he asks, tilting his head to the side.

"One day I'm going to kill you," my voice is weak. "You don't deserve to live."

He laughs before kneeling down. He picks up a pair of pliers from under my chair and clamps them down on one of my toenails.

I struggle, but my restraints are too tight, and so it does nothing.

He rips the nail away, and I howl in agony, fire spreading through my entire foot, blood draining from the painful wound.

He stands and then busts my lip open with his gloved

knuckles. My head swings to the side, my eyes wide and unable to close.

The Reaper pulls a syringe out of his pocket and jabs the needle into the side of my neck before pumping me full of the liquid inside. I struggle violently, but to no avail.

"See you in a few hours, friend," he says before turning around and leaving.

Lazarus is dead is painted across the cement walls, and a loose pipe off to my side is leaking water.

Blood drools from my mouth, footage of my mom taking a bullet to the head plaguing my eyes. I'm numb to it at this point.

Everything around me crumbles into nothing, but I'm still awake.

I want this to end. I want to die.

"Death isn't enjoyable," Simon grabs my chin and forces me to look at him. "You're blind, but you can still hear everything going on around you. You don't want to bite it, trust me."

"I was wondering when you'd show up," I mutter, my hair covering my eyes. "It's been lonely."

He grabs my left hand, glancing down, "They went for the nails, huh?"

I flash him a bloody grin, "Yeah, but the last bastard got too close, and since he wasn't wearing a mask, I bit the top of his ear off."

"Sounds like something you'd do."

"I think I'm losing it, Si. . ."

"You're just realizing that now?"

"I'm scared."

He stares at me for a moment, analyzing, "Of what?"

"I don't even know where to start—"

"You're horrified of being the heir, right? Or maybe it's the fact that you're Mills' slave? Oh, no, I've got it! You're worried that Chloe has a thing for that new kid, right? Wears sunglasses indoors, white hair like he's from some type of comic book?"

I spit blood onto the floor, "No. . ."

"Personally, I'd be more worried about Raph stealing your girl."

"Simon."

He places a hand on my shoulder, "Don't lose your mind in all this, alright? I know this is one crappy situation, but if you just lie down and give up, then everything you know and love will all be done away with."

I grit my teeth, "But how the hell am I supposed to get out of here?"

"Your two weeks down here will be over before you even know it, and then you can start your new job of being the President's lapdog."

"How is that a good thing?"

Hey smirks, his grey eyes prominent in the dark, "Lapdogs are closest to the throat, my friend."

I watch as he turns away and walks into the darkness, and the atmosphere around me falls apart, changing into a completely different scene. My restraints are gone, so I stand from my chair, finding myself in an alleyway that's starting to flood. It's pouring rain, and the brick walls on either side are covered in that horrific face I drew all those months ago.

As I begin to look around, masked figures appear on all sides. They carry pipes and bats in their hands and approach me like fanged predators.

"Get back!" I yell, surrounded and unarmed.

"Die!" one of them shouts.

"You don't deserve to live!" cries another.

"We're going to tear your eyes out!" a third figure blurts.

They simultaneously lunge at me, taking me to the immersed ground. I get kicked, choked, beaten, and ripped apart. I feel the pain, and it's horrendous; the actual seams of my body are torn open, and the water around me turns red.

It all ends when someone shoves a pipe through my eye socket, leaving me to drown in a sea of bloody ink.

Abruptly, my sight returns, and I find myself standing in the middle of the alleyway once more, surrounded on all sides, my assailants all getting ready to strike – but this time, they aren't masked, revealing the faces of those I've killed; Jakob, Marcus, Matthew, and so many others.

Jakob sneers, "Long time, no see, huh doucheface?"

"I'm going to rip your tongue out and make you choke on it," Marcus mutters.

Matthew readies his pipe back, "You're going to pay for what you did to me, Pinder."

He swings, catching me on the side of the face. I collapse to the ground, a groan escaping my lips, everything inside me damaged.

Jakob bends over and stares at me, a knife gripped in his only hand, "Let me do to you what they did to me."

I watch in a daze as he kneels down and pins my left hand down against the asphalt.

My heart pounds against my ribcage. I struggle, but Marcus stomps his foot down on my gut, preventing me from moving.

"Not so fast, freak," he grins.

Jakob begins to saw away at my hand, but instead of pain, I feel rage. . . burning rage that causes my entire body to shake and tremble like an earthquake.

I rip my hand away from the knife, slashing my own wrist in the process. I escape from Marcus' grip by slamming my knuckles against his crotch; he reels away, and I stand up, but a bullet gouges through my skull and splits a hole through my brain.

Everything is suddenly black.

My eyes open, and I'm standing in the middle of the alley again. My attackers are all around me, masked as they were the first time, but I know who they are.

They're my enemies.

I charge one of them, break his kneecap with a swift kick, and rip the pipe out of his hands before jabbing it through his throat. He collapses to the floor, and a primal cry of rage escapes my lips, my eyes wide, my mind feels deranged.

I spend the next few minutes killing every single person around me. Snapping necks, crushing windpipes, beating their faces in with the pipe. When I'm done, the ground is flooded in rainy gore.

My chest heaves up in down, adrenaline the only thing rushing through my veins

"Wanna know what I see?" a voice from behind me asks.

I turn around, seeing the man wearing a metallic morph mask. Vice.

He wears his signature black suit and tie, along with black gloves, slacks, and polished dress shoes.

"What?" I ask. My heart pumps, but my thoughts feel corrupted.

"I see a monster that I've created," he says, clasping his hands behind his back. "And I *love* it."

"Shouldn't you be headless at the morgue getting ready to be burned to ashes right about now?"

His shoulders shake as he laughs; it sounds distorted in my ears, but one thing that's unmistakable is the underlying tone of crazy laced all throughout, "You've found yourself in quite a sticky situation, haven't you, kid? Bomb inside your skull, being brutally tortured, your partners held captive."

I drop the pipe, its impact echoes in the alley, "Is there a point to this conversation?"

"I don't know. . . is there?"

"Get away from me. . . just go."

He turns around, chuckling, and I watch him walk away. Then nothing. Absolutely nothing. Everything's dark.

My vision finally returns and I'm back inside the small room, cuffed to a chair with my eyelids hooked open and the footage of my parents' execution burning through me.

Two Reapers enter in through the door, and for the next three hours, they repeat the same sentence over and over again. I'm so delirious that I don't understand them; they sound incompetent, slurring their words with gibberish.

They beat me, force feed me rotten fruit, then leave as I beg to be shot in the head.

CHAPTER TWENTY-EIGHT

Days go by with nothing. No food, no water, no beatings, nothing. . . nothing but my thoughts.

Since my body isn't injected with the crap that doesn't allow me to sleep, my mind goes blank after a while, and I pass out despite not being able to close my eyes.

Of course, my dreams are nightmares, and I wake up every few hours furious that not even my own brain can give me a break.

Everything is numb inside and out. I can't feel my fingers or my toes, my nose is broken, and my eyes are swollen due to the hooks that force them wide open.

All I can think about is if Mills really thinks that two weeks in this hellhole would hardwire my loyalty to him. He isn't stupid, far from it, so why is he doing this? Why?

I'm missing something, I know I am.

My eyes shift as the door to the room opens, and in walks a Reaper with a key in his hand.

"Times up," he says, but I don't feel any emotion as he unlocks my restraints.

He lifts me up out of the chair and puts me on my feet, but the second he lets go, I crumble to the floor and smack my already broken face against the ground. The hooks that kept my eyes open shatter on impact.

He grunts, picking me back up and forcing me to walk with his arm propped beneath my armpit.

I scream with every step that I take. There's an agonizing sensation springing through my feet.

I look down at my missing toenails and the blood oozing out of the exposed tips whenever I inch forward.

The Reaper escorts me from the room. The torture chamber is dark and damp; doors are everywhere, and it feels like I'm being taken through a barbaric maze. Dry blood stains the walls, nooses hang from the ceiling, and from a room far off to my left, I hear someone howling in agony.

I crumple from the pain that surges through my feet, but the Reaper keeps me up.

"Keep moving," he orders. The modulated voice is the narrator of my nightmares.

I want to say something witty, or even spit all over his gas mask, but I can't. . . not when the two weeks are finally up and I'm able to start the next phase of my plan.

I need to focus on killing Mills and escaping this cesspit with my head intact.

I force my feet to work, and when I have the strength to glance up, I see a showerhead placed on the wall at the back of the corridor. The sight fills me with relief, and I feel my shoulders relax.

For a short time, I was broken, but now I'm fixed.

The Reaper nudges me toward the showerhead, "You have two minutes to wash up."

I steady myself against the wall, "Yes, sir."

I strip my boxers and twist the knob beneath the faucet above. Cool water streams out and purges my body of all the built-up filth.

I lean my head back and gulp down as much fluid as I possibly can.

After my two minutes are up, I turn the water off and fill my lungs with a deep breath of grimy air, my mind already becoming clearer.

Earn his trust, don't question his moves, and be submissive. . . when the time is right, I'll kill the sorry bastard and all those who follow him.

"Good morning, sir," an attractive voice says from behind.

I turn to see two maids in front of me; one of them carries a pair of clothes, and the other holds a sandwich out for me.

Without a second thought, I grab the food out of her hands and devour it within seconds.

One of them giggles, "The President wishes to see you," she pulls a towel out from the stack of clothes and hands it to her friend. "Go dry him off."

I abruptly grab the towel out of her hand, suppressing the glare that begs to be shown, "I'm capable."

They watch as I dry myself off, and the one with clothes steps forward.

"Allow me to help you get dressed," she says with a smile on her face.

I want to deny her, I want to tell her to piss right off, but in all honesty, I don't think I can get dressed on my own. The injuries that litter my body are too much.

"Thank you," I mutter.

A few minutes pass by before I'm dressed up in a servant's uniform, and the other maid combs my hair.

"Hurry," the Reaper demands. "we don't have time to play dress up."

The maid who dressed me glances over at the cold-blooded killer, "President Mills requested that he looked well dressed and groomed."

The Reaper doesn't reply. He stands there with his arms folded across his chest.

Another minute or two passes, and then the two maids leave, presumably pleased with my appearance.

My escort props his arm underneath my armpit as he did before, and the two of us make our way out of the torture chamber. We near the stairs that lead up to the first floor of the Estate when I hear a girl screaming from one of the rooms behind me.

The scream is painfully familiar.

Chloe.

I stop, "It's been two weeks. Why is she still down here?"

"Mills doesn't want your friends out quite yet," he begins leading me up the stairs, and I cringe as shockwaves of electricity surge through my feet. "He's waiting to see if you've changed or not."

Making it up the stairs is horrendous, and as we approach the last few steps, the corners of my vision darken, vividly reminding me of my death.

We make it to the first floor.

"Ah, look," a Reaper who's guarding the front entrance to the Estate, mocks. "It's Prisoner 31103. How are your parents doing, son?"

My eyes widen, and every fiber of my body burns with searing rage.

My fingers begin to twitch violently.

"Looks like you struck a nerve," my escort laughs.

The other entrance guard joins in on the *hilarity*, "Right you are."

I glance over at my escort's holstered knife on his hip. I could grab it and end his life.

But I won't.

Not now, at least.

I'm led to the grand staircase and helped up each step. After we make our way down multiple corridors, we stop in front of the oak door and two guards.

"Prisoner 31103 has a meeting," my escort states.

The two guards nod before stepping out of the way. My attendant then opens the door and takes me inside.

Mills sits behind his desk with a cup of coffee in his hands. He looks at me with a smug, superior grin sweeping across his aging face.

My escort sits me down in an armchair that's directly across from the desk before leaving the room and shutting the door behind him. There's another Reaper in the room; he stares at me with a shotgun held firmly in his grip.

"Two weeks," Mills starts before taking a sip from his mug. "How were they?"

Hellish. Unbearable. Deranged.

"Needed," I say, purposely not making eye contact. "I've seen the error of my ways, and I mean that sincerely, master."

"What errors of yours have you seen?"

"My rebellion. The world can't function without an order like yours, sir. Without you, we'd be a wild and uncontrollable civilization."

He studies me for a moment, "Your words are truly flattering," he pauses, standing from his desk and grabbing his golden cane. He moves to the back of my armchair. "But hear me when I say this," he unsheathes his sword, and I feel the cold metal of its sharp edge up against the side of my throat. "If you so much as give me or anyone else inside my Estate a dirty look, I'll bring you and your friends indescribable pain."

"I understand, sir."

"Good," he pulls the sword away and puts it back inside its sheath. "Because what I have planned for you and your partners is extremely important."

"What do you need? I'll do it for you, sir, anything."

A knock at the door stops him from answering.

He pauses, "What is it?"

"Matthew White has arrived. He wishes to speak with you."

My blood turns to molten lava, and my heart starts pounding like a drum.

Calm down. You need to calm down.

You're a lapdog, remember. . .?

A sinister grin makes its way across Mills' face, "Let him in, we have much to discuss."

The door to the room opens, and my teeth threaten to shatter from how hard I'm gritting them.

Images of Simon flash through my murderous mind; all the memories we shared throughout our friendship burn through me, filling me with unimaginable grief. He was my best friend, the only one who truly understood my motives, the one who tried to keep my thoughts humane.

Well, right now my thoughts consist of utter carnage, and his last words play inside my head over and over again like a broken record.

"No matter what happens, make sure this prick rots in hell. . ."

"Good morning, Matthew," Mills greets. "How are you today?"

"Fine, sir, but I require an assistant for the things you tasked me with. Is there anyone you'd be willing to let me borrow?"

Mills glances over at me before grinning, "Yes. In fact, he's sitting right here."

"Who is it? I can't see him."

"Come take a look."

I hear footfalls approach, then silence.

My eyes narrow to slits, "Matthew," unspeakable wrath clawing at my sanity. "How the hell are ya?"

His one good eye is twitching, *"No, no way! I wouldn't take this freak anywhere other than the morgue!"*

"This is your punishment for going behind my back," Mills says while calmly taking another sip of coffee. "You are to take Jason on all your errands today, and if either of you harms the other, I'll have both of you executed. Do I make myself clear?"

Matthew looks as if he's about to argue, but instead he

chooses to comply, "Get up. We're leaving right now, no questions asked."

My body protests by sending shocks of pain through the nerves, but I stand despite it, "Lead the way."

I follow Matthew out of the office.

"Oh, and Jason," Mills calls out.

I stop, "Yes?"

"Change into something more casual. You've earned it."

I nod before continuing on, my revenge-driven mind fuels my silence as I pass the two Reapers who guard the office.

Again, I think back to Simon's last words.

Don't worry, Si.

I follow Matthew as he turns at the end of the corridor.

I'll make this bastard pay for what he did to you.

CHAPTER TWENTY-NINE

The tension in the air reaches a crescendo as the wheels to the patrol car grind against the off-road trail. The landscape in the outskirts of Seattle is remote. The woods ignore the nearness of civilization and defiantly clutch to their primal essence.

The two of us have been driving for over an hour, and the overhead gloom warns of rain.

Matthew spins the wheel clockwise as we approach the end of the trail, leading us down another path identical to the rest. We continue until we reach the large gate that serves as a blockade.

Two Saints stand in front of the roadblock. Upon seeing Matthew, one punches in a code on a keypad. The gate retracts into the ground, allowing us to drive through.

A clearing the size of two football fields frames a massive facility, resembling a warehouse.

Multiple Saints guard the entrance of the building. The eight of them hold leashes attached to vicious canines. They all look hungry.

Matthew stops the car ten yards away from the entrance, and

without a single word, he exits the vehicle and approaches the guards on duty.

I push my door open and step out. The impact of my feet touching the grass causes my vision to fade black. A spontaneous cuss springs from my lips. I quickly recover my composure, refusing to show the pain. I wait for my vision to return, and I force myself to park at Matthew's side. I keep the desire to kill him from taking over my actions.

"I have important business to attend to on the inside," he tells one of the Saints.

"Understood, sir," the soldier replies. His canine growls restlessly. "But I'm going to need the password before I can let you through."

"Of course," Matthew leans in and speaks inaudibly, covered further by the hounds' snarling.

The Saint nods, then orders his men out of the way. Matthew approaches a keypad mounted on the wall next to the large metal door, and he inputs a lengthy code.

The door unlocks allowing us to enter. The inside is enormous and packed with a many men and women wearing white lab coats. Some of them are working on a device that looks like a grenade, others are in some sort of chemistry station, and most of them are surrounding a massive metal contraption shaped like a sphere. A tall, metal door is centered on a wall meant to close off the device from unwanted eyes. It's open, allowing me to examine their work. Letters and numbers are stenciled across the wall. I focus and make out the sign to say, "The 60d C0d3."

The metal sphere is split down the middle, and inside that space is a see-through vile of yellowish liquid connected to little tubes on each side of the ball.

Matthew walks toward the device, and I follow.

"Ah, Mr. White!" a scientist greets, stepping away from the God Code and approaching us. "What brings you to my lovely facility this fine morning?"

"The President has requested a progress report. As you know, we have a little over two months until our launch date, and Mills is getting antsy."

"Well, do me a favor and tell the president that he has nothing to worry about," the scientist turns to walk away. "If you will follow me, you'll see the test subject that you brought in a few days ago."

Matthew and I follow the man to a wide window that allows us to see into a well-lit room. Near the back lies a corpse sprawled out on the floor. I cringe at the sight of what's left of a face. The eyes are missing, and so are the teeth. The hair is falling out. The skin is grey and has started to rot off the bone.

The corpse wears a Lazarus uniform.

"Wait," I start, feeling my eyes stretch in their sockets. "Who is that?"

Matthew turns to me with a wicked grin on his face, "As I'm sure you're well aware, Lazarus' supply of Rebirth was confiscated. The night we stormed your last facility, we shot and killed many. We suspect this is your friend Marcy McClain." his grin grows wide as my left eye begins to twitch. "Well, Mills told us that we needed a test subject, and she was the only one who didn't get her brain blown out, so we brought her back to life and threw her into this room."

The scientist glances back at me and dryly explains, "We proceeded to expose her to the God Code virus, and this is what's left of her."

My legs give out from under me, and I fall to my knees. I am incapable of keeping the blood from streaming out of my eyes. A metallic smell burns my nostrils.

She didn't deserve this.

Matthew coldly addresses the scientist, "Will it be ready by launch?"

"Of course."

"Good. Now, if you'll excuse me. I have some paperwork to go and get from my office."

"Sounds good to me. Enjoy the rest of your day, sir."

"You too."

Matthew grabs me by the back of the shirt and pulls me to my feet. We walk out of the room. My heart and body throb with grief.

I'm so sorry, Marcy.

We walk to a metal staircase that leads up to the second floor.

About four different sets of stairs later we move down a vast corridor until we approach a door with a name stenciled into it.

He pulls out a set of keys and unlocks it. The inside is spacious and houses a wide desk near the back cluttered in paperwork. A tall lamp stands off to the right, and a single window allows a slight amount of natural light into the room.

Matthew approaches the desk, and I move over to the window. The scenery outside is beautiful as the sky softly drizzles tears from the dark and heavy clouds above. It's a pretty long drop to the ground – maybe eighty feet or so.

The images of Bleach's rotting face stain my eyes and memories. Another dead face added to my collection.

CHAPTER THIRTY

Rain splashes against the windshield. We pull up to a house in the middle of a suburban neighborhood. It's noon, but the overhead gloom gives the appearance of dusk.

Matthew puts the vehicle in park, and the two of us step out.

I want to ask why we're here, but I would rather take a bullet to the head then casually talk to him. He's the reason why I'm here, why my parents are gone, and why my best friend is dead.

Part of me just wants to snap his neck, and even though I'll be killed for it, I'd be at peace with myself.

But I can't leave the others behind. I can't leave Chloe.

Never.

We step up to the front door, and he knocks.

"Who is it?" someone from the inside calls.

"It's Matthew."

"Oh, I'll be right there."

We wait a few moments before the door opens, and I'm surprised to see a kind looking young brunette with soft eyes. She appears to be my age – maybe just a bit older. She wears a grey sweatshirt and sweatpants.

"How're you doing, Abigail?" Matthew greets.

"I'm doing fine, how about you?" she greets back.

"I've been better," he pauses. "Your uncle sent me."

She's smiling, but it briefly falters, "Oh, why? Is everything okay?"

"Of course, of course. It's just a wellness check."

"Promise?"

"Yes, I promise. Mind if we come in?"

"Yeah, sure."

She moves out of the way and lets us enter, closing the door behind us. She takes us to the living room and invites us to sit down on one of the couches.

"Would you two like anything to drink?" she asks, and I can sense her anxiety.

"What do you have?" Matthew asks.

"Lemonade, tea, and water. Oh, and milk if you want."

"Surprise me."

"And what about your partner there?"

The two of us exchange glares, and I would be lying if I said that I didn't want to use the sewing needle that's on the end table next to me to jab out his other eye.

He gradually looks away, but I notice that he doesn't let go of his hip holster, "He's good, thanks though."

A minute of silence passes, and Abigail reenters the room with a glass of lemonade in one hand, and a cup of tea in the other, "Sorry for the wait. Here."

She hands Matthew the lemonade and sits down on the couch opposite to us.

"Thanks," he takes a sip. "So, how's your boy?"

Abigail brings the cup of tea up to her lips, "He's doing wonderful. He's at a friend's house for the day – I needed to get some cleaning done, and he's starting to teethe so I haven't been able to do much other than comfort him."

"Teething babies are the worst. Back when my little girl was one," he stops, and his hands begin to tremble ever so slightly.

"Sorry, I'm wasting time. Listen, your uncle wants to know how you've been mentally. Any mood swings, or suicidal thoughts?"

Abigail seems to be taken aback, "Pardon?"

"I know these are personal questions, but I need an honest answer."

"Mr. White, you're kind of scaring me."

"Just answer, and then we can move on."

"No, no I haven't."

"How have you been handling your husband's death? You two had only been married for a year before his car crash last month."

Her eyes go misty, "Can you please just tell me why my uncle needs to know these things?"

"I'm not allowed to disclose the reasoning."

The tension in the room rises.

My shoulders tense up a bit.

Abigail sighs, "It's been rough, and you know that."

"You graduated at the top of your class, have no history of mental illness, and are a wonderful mother. This is exactly why he picked you."

I raise an eyebrow, but keep my mouth shut.

"Picked me?" Abigail asks, her face growing paler and paler. "What do you mean by that?"

Matthew stands, "The two of us need to get going."

She stands as well, "Mr. White, you never answered my ques—"

Matthew jabs her in the side of the neck with a syringe. She lets out a little yelp, then collapses to the floor, spilling tea all over the white carpet.

He bends over and picks her up. Without even shooting me a glance, he leaves the house. A million thoughts run through my mind.

What was she picked for? Why did her mental status determine anything?

I stand from the couch and follow my rival.

CHAPTER THIRTY-ONE

bigail's body swings limply in Matthew's arms as the two of us approach the Reapers guarding the entrance of the Estate. Once we're a few feet away, one of them asks Matthew for a password.

"Eden."

The two of them step to the side, and Matthew uses his free hand to open one of the doors. I follow behind him, sensing that my socks are soaked in blood. My absent toenails leave the tips of my feet surging in unreserved agony. I feel like I need constant support, so the second I enter the building I lean up against the solid wall.

Matthew leaves me when two maids approach.

"Sir, please strip your clothing," one of them say, and she wears a patient look.

I reluctantly do as I'm told, pulling off my white long sleeve shirt and tossing it to one of them before unzipping my blue jeans.

After I'm scrutinized in my boxers, they assist me in getting redressed.

"I'm capable of doing this myself, you know that, right?" I mutter as one of them puts a dress shirt over me.

"We know, but we have to make sure that you aren't smuggling any weapons," says the maid, sliding black slacks up my legs.

"What could I possibly use as a weapon?" I ask.

"A lot of things," the first one remarks. "You *are* second in command for a terrorist organization."

"*Was*," I correct.

They don't reply, instead they finish their task of dressing me.

They then quickly rush me to a dining hall. In the center of the spacious room, a large table with a red velvet table cloth draped over is encircled by what remains of Lazarus along with Mills. I find myself clamoring for Chloe's eye contact, assuring me that she is alright. She is reluctant to give me anything but a brief glance.

Mills' seat resembles a throne, and a smile sweeps across his face when he sees me, "I'm glad to see that you behaved yourself. Come take a seat."

Chloe shifts in her seat and pushes the hair out of her eyes. She looks defiant and strong. The sight of her fills with me with renewed energy, and I'm happy to see that she isn't letting the torture she endured rattle her.

I sit in the empty chair next to her. The aroma of cooked meat is heavy in the air. I allow my shoulders to slightly relax.

"Dig in," Mills commands.

The roast on my plate is covered in juices that bleed into the bottom of a serving of mashed potatoes. My stomach has been growling for hours, so I begin to devour the meal like an animal, not caring how rude I look. I finish my meal within a minute, then wash it down with the provided red wine, using the napkin that was given to me to wipe my face in one swipe.

Mills stares at me with a devilish grin on his face. His eyes remain dark and quizzical. The desire to tell him to piss off builds up inside, but it stops when Chloe grabs my hand. My bloody fingertips are still very sore and the action forces a jolt of pain to surge through my arm.

I abruptly pull away.

"Sorry," I mutter, quickly wiping my eyes before any crimson can escape.

"What's wrong?" she whispers.

I squint over at her before pulling the glove off my left hand, revealing the disturbing sight.

She gawks, "What did they do to you?"

"A lot."

"Did they do something to your face? You're wearing sunglasses at night, indoors."

I bring a hand up to my face and twitch the dark shades down a bit, showing off the purplish-blue bruising around both of my eyes caused by the hooks and beatings.

"They didn't touch me," she says. I sit stunned, remembering the cries I heard in the dungeon. The sound of everyone eating masks her explanation. "All they did was inject me with this hallucinatory drug – the same one they used back in Salem."

I tilt my shades back up, "I was worried about you."

Mills clears his throat, "Why don't you tell us about your day, Jason?"

The fact that he expects me to converse with him makes my blood boil, but I force all of the scorching hatred out through my unsteady breaths, "We went out to a facility in the woods; saw some interesting tech, and then we stopped by some woman's house."

"Oh, Abigail? How did that go?"

Matthew stabbing her in the neck with a needle flashes through my head, and I pause, "Fine."

"Good," he stops to take a bite out of his roast. "As you can see, your partners have been let out of my chamber, and they all have made the same choice that you have, serving me with the utmost amount of loyalty. Before we truly get started on this newfound beginning, I have one last surprise for you all."

Raphael has been quiet this entire time, until now. He looks up from his plate, "Which is?"

Mills claps his hands together twice, and one of the Reapers watching over the dinner briefly disappears through the door leading into what I assume to be the kitchen.

We hear a struggle, a scream, and then silence.

Something is thrown through the kitchen door and into the dining hall.

Kennedy. He helped me blow up the military hospital back in New Jersey. Other members are thrown out; Ross, then Sam, and finally Cass. They all have gags in their mouths, and their hands are cuffed behind their backs.

"As you can see," Mills starts, his voice reeking of triumph. "I had the four Lazarus members who blew up one of my hospitals detained."

Cass screams for help, but it's muffled. Her mascara runs down her cheeks.

"No, please," I beg, looking at Mills with wide, pleading eyes. "They can change their ways – they'll be loyal to you, all of them!"

"Jason, I want you to stand," he says.

I do as I'm told.

"Now, walk over to your four friends."

Again, I do as I'm told, limping in the process. All eyes are on me.

"Pick two to live. You have one minute."

My heart drops, "What?"

"If you don't, then all of them will die."

The Reaper steps out of the kitchen and aims his shotgun at the back of Kennedy's head.

Raphael stands from his chair, "You can't do this!"

Another Reaper in the room aims his weapon at Raphael, "Shut the hell up, skull face."

Raphael turns, his eyes emitting unspeakable rage, "What did you just call me?"

Mills clasps his hands on the table, "I would sit down before you get hurt, Mr. Ramirez."

He waits a moment before slowly taking a seat. His hands tremble, and his knuckles fade white.

Mills turns to me, "As I was saying, you have a minute . . . starting now."

Sweat drips down my forehead, my frame shakes, and my stomach knots up, "But, sir—"

He ignores me and begins to count down from sixty,

I stare down at my fellow insurgents. Ross' brow is furrowed, Kennedy's eyes are wide and filled with terror, Sam is emotionless, and Cass has tears streaming down her flushed cheeks.

What do I do?

Seconds upon seconds pass and all I can do is stare down at the people who look up to me as a leader. My mind is crumbling.

Who do I pick?

"Twenty-five, twenty-four, twenty-three—"

I tune Mills out, and focus on fortifying my weak knees.

Kennedy manages to loosen his gag, "Jason! Jason please!"

The Reaper behind him slams the butt of his shotgun into the back of his head. He falls forward, and then is told to shut his mouth.

Ross struggles violently, but it doesn't do a thing.

Cass continues to cry.

Sam shows no expression.

"Ten, nine, eight—"

Why me? Why do I have to decide?

"Four, three, two—"

"*These two!*" I blurt, pointing at Kennedy and Cass. "*Keep these two alive!*"

Mills nods, "As you wish."

He snaps his fingers, and I watch in terror as the Reaper aims his shotgun at the back of Ross' head and fires. Cass screams as Sam meets the same fate, his blood staining her face.

My heart bursts in unbearable pain, and I collapse to my knees. Blood streams from my eyes and stains my clothes.

A pathetic cry of anguish escapes my lips.

"I didn't know you were so vulnerable when it came to people dying," Mills states, leaning back in his chair a bit. Looking over at the executioner, he orders. "Take the two deceased members of Lazarus down to the incinerator."

The Reaper grabs Sam and Ross by their ankles and drags them out of the dining hall. Mills orders the other Reaper to un-gag and uncuff Kennedy and Cass so that they can be seated and eat.

I watch as they are escorted to two empty chairs alongside the large dining table.

"One last thing," Mills tells his bodyguard. "Could you help Jason to his seat?"

He nods, grabbing me by the collar and hoisting me up.

CHAPTER THIRTY-TWO

I stare up at the ceiling in the bedroom while the parasite of guilt eats me alive from the inside-out.

I listen to the rhythmic beep inside my head.

I was the cause of two innocent deaths. It's all my fault.

I reach up and tug at my hair with both hands. A growl reverberates from my throat.

Lazarus has been defeated, and nothing can change that. What remains of the organization is trapped inside this place of torment with bombs planted inside our heads. We're ensnared. Mills owns us. I want him to press the button that will rupture my entire skull.

No. You don't want that. You have too much to live for.

That's a lie.

The door to my room opens to a Reaper.

Why is a Reaper here? What else does this night have in store for me? Can't I just get a break?

I quickly stand from my bed, "What do you want?"

To my surprise, he shuts the door behind him, "Listen, I don't have a lot of time – that camera over there is only going to be off for two minutes, so listen, and listen very carefully."

I raise an eyebrow and look to see a red light blinking on the camera instead of the usual green.

"My name is Leviticus, and I'm here to help get you and the others out of here alive."

"Wait, what?"

"The escape is going to happen in just a few days, so I need you to be a *perfect* little angel for Mills so that he won't send you back down to the chamber. Tell the others the same, and leave the rest up to me, got it?"

I don't trust him, "Why help us? What's in it for you?"

He pauses for a moment, "Because just like you, I lost everything close to me, and I want revenge. You and your friends are just one of the many steps that I need to take to ensure that I get it."

"And how am I supposed to trust you? You're a Reaper."

"I'm not who you think I am, trust me."

"Then who are you?"

"You'll know when the time is right."

He turns around, and I watch him leave, shutting the door behind him.

I watch the camera until the green light next to the lens flashes back on.

What if this is some ploy orchestrated by Mills to catch me in the act of betraying him? This is too good to be true, but what if? What if he really does want to help us escape?

Does Mills think that I'll sympathize with Leviticus and go along with his mutinous plan? Or is this actually real?

What the hell is going on?

I sit back down on my bed, and listen to the faint beeping from inside my head. Even if I do escape, what am I going to do about the bomb inside me? Mills' remote also needs to be destroyed.

I already know where the God Code is, and I know how to get in. If I can escape, I can shut it down, and then everyone won't end up like Bleach. Chloe will be safe.

I pause for a moment, and for the first time since being captured, I feel some sort of hope blossoming from inside my chest.

"Kinda fishy," Simon says, sitting down at the foot of my bed. "Don't you think?"

"Of course it is," I mutter, and without looking at him, I step over to the two glass doors that lead out to the balcony and stare up at the black, gloomy sky. "But what other choice do I have?"

"I guess you're right. It's either you trust him, and maybe make it out of here alive, or don't trust him, and get wiped out by the God Code when it goes off. . . Oh, by the way, your girl was looking *fine* in that short little skirt earlier."

Ignoring him, I continue staring up at the sky, and guilt begins to tear through me again. "Sam and Ross' deaths aren't my fault, are they?"

There's no reply.

"Are they, Si?" I ask once more, my voice cracking.

I turn, and nobody is there.

CHAPTER THIRTY-THREE

Despite the pain bursting through my feet, I walk with purpose alongside my escort – the same maid who fetched me for the first time two weeks back. She's taking me to Mills for reasons that are unknown to me, but I don't care. My mind is full of intricate plans that consist of escape and revenge.

So much of me feels that Leviticus is a fraud, but I feel myself longing to believe him. Even if he's lying, I won't let myself just rot away in the Estate working for a sociopath who thinks he can play God.

I'm getting us all out of here one way or another; even if that means the contents of my skull getting splattered.

"You've never told me your name," I casually state as my escort leads me up a flight of stairs.

"And why would I?" she shoots back, her voice remaining soft.

"Common courtesy?"

"It's Autumn."

"Pretty name."

She ignores me. We reach the top of the stairs, and she leads me down a couple of corridors, stopping in front of Mills' office. She orders the two Reapers to let me enter.

"The President has requested his presence," she says, her shoulders remaining tense.

One of them nods, "Very well."

They both step out of the way, and Autumn turns to leave as I turn the golden knob. The hinges swivel back. Mills sits behind his desk with his cane gripped in his right hand.

"Come take a seat," he greets, ushering me to the armchair in front of his desk.

The Reaper in the room stares at me through un-seeable eyes as I sit down, his weapon held in his solid grip. It's quiet for a moment, and then Mills slurps a sip from his coffee mug.

"How did you sleep?" he asks.

"Fine, thank you for asking, sir."

"Of course. Did you enjoy dinner last night?"

Sam and Ross getting their brains blown to bits by a shotgun blast streaks in my mind, but I quickly push the ghosts away, "The wine was a bit austere."

He laughs, "Oh, it was? My apologies," he sets his mug down and continues groping the handle to his cane. "Listen, Jason, I have something lined up for you and your friends this morning."

"Which is what?"

"I know we've settled our differences, but you are still the ex-heir of Lazarus, and because of that fact, I'm going to have you and your surviving members star in a little public announcement. Your friends are already in my throne room awaiting your arrival. You will be given your lines as we go, and failure to comply will result in harsh punishments, do I make myself clear?"

The rage pulses in rhythm to the beeping in my skull, "Yes, sir."

THE THRONE ROOM IS SPACIOUS BUT FEELS CROWDED with the film crew. The man operating the camera has his lens trained on the remaining Lazarus members, and there's a teleprompt off to the side that shows us our lines; my mind won't cooperate and unjumble the mess of letters. The warning I was given earlier rings through my head as sweat dots my forehead.

Mills sits in his extravagant black throne with a wide smile across his face and his cane in his grip, "Who do you serve, Mr. Ramirez?"

Raphael's body trembles, but he relaxes just long enough to say, "You, and only you, sir."

Mills grins even wider, "And what about you, Mr. West?"

Exodus' expressionless face answers, "You, of course."

"And you, Ms. Frye?"

Chloe's teeth are gnashed, her eyes narrow to slits, and her fists shake at her sides, "You."

Mills continues down the line, asking both Cass and Kennedy the same thing before getting to me, "Jason Pinder, who do you serve?"

I glance over at the teleprompt, but can't read anything, "You, sir."

He stares at me a moment, and then stands from his throne and approaches Raphael, asking him if he's still loyal to Lazarus.

"What's Lazarus?" Raphael asks.

Mills shrugs, "I don't know," he turns to Exodus. "Do you know who Lazarus is, son?"

"No, sir, I don't know who that is."

"And you, Ms. Frye, do you know who Lazarus is?"

Chloe shakes her head, her eyebrows furrowed, "No idea, sir."

He asks us all the same question, and we all give the same answers. We then kneel before him, and the cameras turn off.

"Bravo," one of the Reapers slowly claps his hands. "You all almost looked like you meant it."

Raphael turns to him, "We do."

Mills turns to his throne as the camera crew begins moving

equipment around, "You six did well. Head down to the dining hall for some breakfast. We'll get more footage afterward."

We nod, and the Reapers in the room escort us out. As we exit one by one, I look through the large window that fills the east wall. The sun rises through the beautiful morning sky.

I'm shoved out the door.

CHAPTER THIRTY-FOUR

The rest of the day is spent shooting more public *announcements*. Some of them were similar to the one we shot before breakfast. They all made my blood boil.

I'm lying in my bed with my dress shirt untucked, my tie partially undone and hanging off to the side, and my shoes off.

The quiet beeping sound coming from my head assures me that the bomb inside my skull is still fully operational. I slap my forehead, but it does nothing. I repeat the smacking until there's a knock at my door.

"Come in," I mutter.

The door opens, and my stomach flutters at the sight of Chloe. Her gorgeous emerald green eyes flicker as they meet mine.

"What're you doing here?" I ask, my heart thumping a little harder than usual.

I haven't been alone with Chloe since coming to the Estate. I've missed it more than anything, but I can't help being suspicious about the visit. How did she manage to get to me?

She shuts the door behind her, "Mills said that I could come see you since we've both been *obedient*, but I only have a few minutes, plus an escort is coming to monitor the two of us. "

I sit up, "Okay, just make sure you don't say anything sensitive," I point over to the camera in the room, but raise an eyebrow as I see that there's a red light next to the lens instead of green, signifying that it's off.

"What's with the face?" she asks, approaching the bed before taking a seat next to me.

I look over at her, shaking away my confusion, "It's nothing, don't worry about it."

She sighs, "What do you think's going to happen to us? The God Code is going off in two months, and there's nothing we can do about it if we're stuck in this place."

I want to tell her about Leviticus, but the fear of my room having been bugged with hidden mics stops me, "It's going to be fine, I promise."

She leans in to kiss my neck, but instead whispers, "Jason, we have to get out of here."

I stare at her for a moment, and the next thing I know, our lips are pressed together. All worries escape from my mind, and I push her down, one hand on her thigh, the other on her hip. Her lips are warm, and her cheeks are burning just like mine.

I care about her more than anyone, and the thought of her dying makes me hold onto her even tighter. My chest heaves with emotion.

She softly pushes me away, "Jason— Jason, hold on."

I stop, "What's wrong?"

"We're being held hostage with bombs inside our heads. . . we need to stay focused."

"But—"

"Later."

The door to my room opens to a Reaper.

"Sorry for interrupting," he says, entering and shutting the door behind him. "I only have two minutes before the camera turns back on again."

I get off of Chloe, forcing my desire away, "Leviticus?"

"In three days, Mills is going to have you come alone to the throne room to shoot another thing for his propaganda. As you know, you'll have to be checked before filming, and I'll make sure that I'm the one to do it – that way, I can place a knife in your hand."

Chloe sits up, readjusting her clothes, "Who's this?"

"The name's Leviticus," he looks over at me. "Haven't you told her about the plan?"

"Not yet," I reply, fixing my shirt. "There hasn't been a good time."

"Listen, you did great today, and you didn't get into any trouble. Keep it up, and in three days, we'll be out of here, and most importantly, Mills will be dead."

"But how am I supposed to get close enough to kill him? There will be more than just you who's guarding him, I'm sure."

"Don't doubt me, kid. I know how the system works, you don't."

"How do I know that this isn't just some messed up attempt at trying to get me caught for betraying Mills and attempting to escape? How can I trust you? I know that the elites have mics embedded into their uniforms, and you, my friend, are an elite."

Leviticus waits a moment before reaching up with both hands and pulling off his gas mask.

A million thoughts enter my mind as I stare into the eyes of the unveiled soldier, "No way."

He swiftly puts it back on, securing it to his face before turning around, "Don't doubt me again, and make sure that you prepare yourself mentally for what's to come," he reaches for the doorknob. "Get some rest, Jason," he pauses upon opening the door. "Oh, and I had all my mics destroyed – blamed it on a programming error."

He leaves.

"Wait, who is that? Do you know him?" Chloe asks.

"Julie." I say, hardly able to get any words out.

"Julie? Who's Julie?"

"Do you remember how Simon talked about his girlfriend?"

"Yeah, why?"

"That Reaper is her dad."

CHAPTER THIRTY-FIVE

W arm water sputters from the shower head above,
splashing against my naked body.

Last night was absolutely insane. Julie Briggens' dad? What is
he doing here? How is he a Reaper? Why does he want revenge?
Do we have the same goals?

I can't believe that this is actually happening. Anxiety is
bursting through my veins, and the three-day countdown has
already started inside my head. I don't know how he's going to
pull it off, but I trust Mr. Briggens.

In my mind, I'm already out of the Estate and recruiting more
members to help me and the other survivors shut down the God
Code. I picture us storming the facility.

I picture us overthrowing The President.

I was told before I got into the shower that Mills wanted to
meet with me as soon as possible, so I finish up and step out. I
towel myself dry, get dressed into my uniform – minus the tie –
and step out of the bathroom.

Autumn greets me and puts on my tie before escorting me over
to Mills' office. She tells the two Reapers on guard that Mills'

requested my presence, and they step out of the way without question.

She turns around, and I enter.

"Good morning, Jason," Mills greets with a coffee mug in his hand. "Come take a seat, I have a special guest who is coming in to talk to me about some private information, and I want you to hear it."

"Why, sir?"

"Because I want to see the look on your face."

A knock on the door gives me the chance to take a breath.

"Come in," Mills orders.

I turn to see Matthew enter, "Thank you for meeting with me, I just—" he stops as he sees me, his one good eye filling with wrath. "What is *he* doing here?"

Mills sets his mug down, "I wanted him to hear our little conversation."

"But sir!"

"I don't want to hear it, Matthew."

I watch with bliss as Matthew has to forcibly calm himself down, "As you wish. . . As you know, I wanted to have a meeting with you about Operation Eden. I still have some concerns that I wanted to run by you," he looks directly at me, "if that's okay."

Mills nods before leaning back in his chair, "Of course, but first, I want you to explain Operation Eden to Jason before you begin listing your concerns."

"You can't be serious, sir."

"Oh, but I am. I want to see the look on his face."

"As you wish," he gulps, and a vein pops out in his forehead, "Operation Eden ties in with the God Code. After we wipe out all civilization in the world – minus a select few – Mills plans on starting over; a new world where everyone looks to him as a God – which he is."

I have to stop myself from clenching my fists, "But why?"

He glares at me, "Don't question us."

Mills sits up a bit, "As I'm sure you're well aware, I've had to deal with a lot of revolts and uprisings lately. Lazarus was the last straw, and I had the God Code built. You were with Matthew when he abducted my niece, Abigail, correct?"

I nod, not uttering a word.

"Yes, well think of her as the new Eve. She will be one of the few women who will help repopulate this country, baring me children who will worship me, and who will not partake in any mutinies."

You crazy bastard.

Matthew steps forward a bit, "Sir, may I begin listing my concerns."

"Why yes, of course."

"Everyone else has a partner but Abigail; who's going to be the new Adam?"

I stop Mills' reply, "If you're just going to kill everyone, then why are you keeping me and the others alive? Why are you shooting videos to convince the public of your supremacy?"

He stares at me for a moment, "Because there's unrest in America. People are growing more rebellious by the day, and at any moment, there could be a snapping point. I captured you and your friends, the most notorious insurgents in my society to show the public that I own you. Their thoughts of an uprising are suppressed. You failed, and that scares them. I just need enough time for the God Code to finish, and then on Christmas Eve, I will have it set off and everyone but myself and a select other few will die."

"I'm guessing your soldiers aren't too happy about that," I say, an expressionless look on my face.

The Reaper in the room looks at me, "We are all willing to die for the president."

Mills grins, "Exactly."

I turn to Matthew, befuddled, "And what about you? You're just gonna up and die?"

He lets out a sinister grin, "I'm one of the select few who gets to live."

CHAPTER THIRTY-SIX

As I lie on my bed, my mind recalls the uneventful days that have passed since I was told about Operation Eden. We shot more videos, I told the others about the escape plan, my toes have finally stopped hurting as bad, and my pounding headaches have subsided.

My mind wanders back further, recalling both wanted and unwanted memories. I see flashes of my death, of Fight-Night, of my revenge. More than anything else, the memories of all those I've killed cause a chain reaction of agony, regret, and anger to pulse through my body.

You've done what you've had to do.

That's a lie. You're a murderer.

No, I'm overthrowing a tyrannical government run by someone who's goal is to commit mass genocide.

Saints aren't people, right?

There's a knock at my door, and Autumn presents a pressed uniform, "The President has requested you up to the throne room."

"What for?" I ask despite already knowing the answer.

She steps closer and sets the uniform on the bed, "Another filming – he says that this will be the last one."

I suppress the grin forming on my lips.

You have no idea how true that is.

I step out of bed and dress in my uniform.

"Would you like help with your tie?" she asks me.

"Yes, please."

She steps forward, looping the black tie around my collar and tying it in a double Windsor. I think of all the times my dad and I got into arguments over my incompetent knot tying. He would tell me to put in the effort to learn, and I always blew him off, using my mental disability as an excuse.

After Autumn's done, she fixes my hair and escorts me out of my room for the last time. In the hallway, I glance around, looking at the walls that are adorned with pictures, clocks, and other priceless items. I study the chandeliers above, telling myself over and over again that I'm about to be free and Mills is about to meet an untimely demise.

I glance down at my gloved hands, hoping that the absence of fingernails won't slow me down too much. For the first two or so days, it hurt like hell to grab anything, but now it's just a dull buzz. The gloves are used to prevent infection, which I found ironically courteous of the staff here at the Estate. I can't help but think they just don't want to see the hideous result of their methods.

My eyes meet a large painting at the end of the next hall. It's a portrait of Mills. He looks a bit younger in the painting, and he's sitting in an antique looking armchair with a curly haired woman standing at his side.

"Who's the chick in the painting?" I ask.

"The president's late wife. She died a long time ago during one of the riots that took place after Mills took his third term. I wouldn't mention her, though. The topic is sensitive for the President."

"What was her name?"

"Chantelle. From what I hear, she was an amazing woman."

We continue down the hall, and after a few moments, we find ourselves on the grand staircase. The red velvet carpet that covers each step is the same shade as blood. Each floor has a break where you can step off the staircase. We exit at the top floor and come to a stop in front of a large, cherry-colored, oak door and two Reapers standing guard.

They carry tactical shotguns with jet black bayonets attached to the ends. Their ominous gas masks appear darker than usual in the fluorescent lighting above.

"State your business," one of them orders.

Autumn bows her head, "The President has requested Jason's presence for another filming."

"Very well."

The two guards step out of the way, and I enter the throne room. The full moon outside the massive window is poised high in the sky. The room is well lit. There are four Reapers standing guard, the film crew is stationed and ready, and there are a few maids who are hand-feeding Mills grapes while he sits in his charred throne.

"Good evening, Jason," he greets before another grape is placed in his mouth.

"Good evening, sir."

"Are you ready for your last film?"

"Of course, sir."

"Kneel where you stand."

I comply, getting down on one knee with one hand tucked behind my back.

Mills looks around the room at the Reapers, "One of you, check him for weapons."

I look up, "Sir, you should know by now that I have no plans on rebelling."

He ignores me and snaps his fingers. One of the Reapers

approaches me from behind; he pats me down, and relief fills my stomach when I feel the grip of a knife in my hand. I quickly become comfortable with the weight of the blade.

Mr. Briggens hasn't let me down.

Mills snaps once more, "Start the camera, and make sure the footage is being broadcast to every screen across the nation, understand?"

Some of the crew nod, and out of the corner of my eye, I see the teleprompt turn on.

"Who do you serve?"

"You, master."

"Who are you loyal to?"

"You, master."

He gradually stands from his throne, stepping closer to me with his golden cane firmly in his grasp. The air in the room is thick with tension, and he asks, "How do you feel about Lazarus?"

I grip the knife tighter, "What's Lazarus?"

He stops in front of me, "Who owns you?"

I glance around the room, my heart beating out of my chest. Three out of the four Reapers in the room are aiming their weapons at me. Mr. Briggens and I are outgunned.

Despite the fear in my mind, and the churning in my stomach, I answer, "You do."

He steps closer, and I note how the three guards have their fingers wrapped around their triggers.

I breathe, breathe some more. My thoughts are messy and scattered.

"Despite your profound loyalty, you still have committed unpardonable acts of violence toward me and my people," he says. The air in the room grows thicker and thicker. "For that, you must die, and you will do nothing about it because I *own* you."

My eyes widen as he slowly unsheathes his sword from the cane-scabbard. I jump to my feet and slash as fast as I can. The blade slides across his throat, and his flesh splits open, blood spurting from it like a geyser.

His eyes bulge out of his skull.

Mr. Briggens turns to the other three Reapers and pulls the trigger, spraying bullets into the guards. The holes penetrate their masks.

Two maids approach Mills and scream as he grasps his throat with both hands, gurgling. I move to finish the job, but the door to the throne room bursts open, and the two guards from outside rush in.

Mr. Briggens shoots one of them in the face, but the other squeezes the trigger to his shotgun, sending a fiery blast of pellets into the air. I turn my head just in time to see Julie's dad get his hand shredded from the impact of the shot. The protective armor guards his vital organs.

He screams and collapses to the floor, and the Reaper aims his weapon at me. My entire body tenses up, and I prepare to take the blast, but the massive window behind me shatters, and gunfire erupts.

The Reaper takes a group of bullets to the face and chest. Blood stains the open door next to him and slides down the oak fixture.

Tommy's dressed in tactical gear and carries a gun in his hand. I flinch as he fires another round.

I look just in time to see Mills hobbling out of the throne room, one of the maids who's escorting him takes a bullet to the head, splintering her skull.

Tommy swears, and I sprint after the President, but he quickly pulls me back.

"What are you doing?" I ask, the knife held loosely in my grip.

"We don't have much time," he mutters, looking down at Mr. Briggens. "Take him and get him to the white van that's parked out front."

My mind is frantic, "What are you going to go do?"

"We have the others in on the plan; I'm going to go help where I can."

"Do you know where Chloe is?"

"If she followed through, then she'll be in the security department, cutting all the footage."

Two more Reapers enter the room, and one of them sends a bullet into Tommy's chest. He flinches back before aiming up and pulling the trigger numerous times. They collapse to the floor.

Tommy shoves me toward Mr. Briggens, "Go," he tells me. "Get Dante out of here and down to the van. There's a rope hanging out of the window; use it to transport him"

I nod, and he rushes out of the throne room and down the corridor.

Mr. Briggens is trying to keep calm, but I can sense his urgency, "Get this mask offa me."

I clasp my hands around the gas mask and tug it off before tossing it to the ground, "Can you stand?"

He sits up, cringing in the process, "I'll need some help, kid."

I nod, wrapping my arms around him and pulling him to his feet. He stumbles. Blood drips from his obliterated hand. The tactical armor covering his torso ripped up, but intact. With his good hand, he reaches into his pocket, pulling out a pill bottle and downing three of the capsules inside. I recognize the Aburaek. The meds numb all pain in the body.

I help him over to the shattered window, and quickly find the black rope hanging from the roof above.

"How am I supposed to get you down? You don't have a hand."

He winces, "Don't you think I know that?"

I step on the windowsill, grabbing a hold of the rope, "Come on, I'll carry you."

He shakes his head, "No, go on ahead, I'll be right behind you."

"But how? Your hand. . . you can barely move."

"Trust me, I'll be fine. I'm more than capable."

I hesitate, but I do as he wishes, gripping the rope tightly and stepping off the sill. My gloves heat up as I slide down, and when I reach the bottom, Mr. Briggens grabs hold of the rope and makes his way down.

I prop an arm under him, and the two of us sprint across the front lawn of the Estate while gunfire continues to erupt from inside the mansion.

"Jason, grab the handgun out of my hip holster, and follow my lead."

I unholster his weapon, "Got it."

Two Reapers rush toward us. Their trench coats sway in the wind, and their guns are drawn.

"Hold your fire!" Mr. Briggens orders. Blood spills from his wounds, staining the freshly cut grass. The metallic smell clouds my nostrils. "There's been an attack. The President had his throat slit by a maid, and then some of the Lazarus members came in and started shooting up the place."

One of them points his gun directly at my face, "I knew Mills was a fool for letting them live."

"No, but this one saved me. He's loyal," Mr. Briggens insists.

Both guards lower their guns, and one of them asks, "But how can you be sure?"

I abruptly raise my gun up to his face, "Gut feeling."

I fire a round into his face before swaying the barrel over to his partner and putting a bullet through his skull. The two of them collapse, and Mr. Briggens and I continue running. The white van is in sight.

"What about the bomb in my head?" I ask.

"Don't worry about that."

"Why not?"

"Just keep moving."

I don't argue, sprinting despite the beeping inside my skull.

We make it to the van, and he slides the side door open, letting me help him inside. Once the two of us are situated, I slide the door shut, sweat pouring down my face. My white dress shirt is stained with Mills' blood.

Is he still alive?

A scream bursts from my lips as a needle is jabbed into my neck. Mr. Briggens pumps me full of some liquid before ripping the syringe out.

"What was that?"

"It'll disarm the bomb. The liquid dissolves the shell before eating away at the rest of the explosive.'

A huge sigh of relief escapes my chest, "Thank you, Mr. Briggens."

"It's Dante. No need to be so formal."

I glance down at his wound, "You're bleeding like crazy, what do you want me to do?"

"Rip off some of that suit coat you're wearing and wrap it around my wrist."

I nod, taking off my jacket and grabbing the knife attached to his belt. I cut off a strip of fabric and wrap it around his wrist. The bleeding slows down.

"What now?" I ask.

"We wait. Tommy has five other people he needs to rescue without dying."

"Should I head back inside and help?"

"That would be a death sentence."

"But what if—"

"No, Jason, just stop. Worrying about them isn't going to do a single thing. Just wait here like we were told to do, and when they get here, they get here."

I stay silent for a moment, "So, what happened to you? Why do you want to play the sweet game of revenge?"

He looks at me for a moment, his eyes cold and dark, "They killed my wife and daughter."

My eyes widen and my heart stammers, "They killed Julie?"

He slowly nods, "Shot her in the back of the head."

My bottom lip quakes, "But why? Why wasn't she brought back to life like the rest of us?"

"I don't know, Jason."

"And why didn't they kill you too? Mills had Brookhaven wiped out because of the laws that were being broken. They were going to go after Tommy, but he faked his own death."

"Jason, I don't know."

Blood fills my eyes, "Why the hell did they have to do this to us? Why did they have to take everything away from me? From you?"

"Because Mills thinks he can play God," he stops for a moment. "We're gonna be the end of him and his government, Jason. We're gonna shut down the God Code, kill every last Saint and Reaper and stop him."

"I slit his throat. He's done."

"Don't be so sure of that."

"What do you mean?"

"The government still has their hands on Rebirth, or whatever you call it."

Blood trails down my cheeks, "Well good. It'll just give me another opportunity to finish him, but this next time, we'll make sure that he can never come back."

Both doors up front open, and I see Tommy get behind the wheel while Raphael buckles himself up.

The side door to the van slides open, and I desperately look for Chloe as the Lazarus members climb in. She's the last in line, and I'm instantly relieved.

I can't do any of this without her.

Tommy takes off the second everyone's seated. I flinch when I hear the bullets hit the back of the van. One enters and misses my face by just an inch or two, slamming into the dash up front.

Dante hands me another syringe out of his pocket, "Inject them. Hurry."

I jab Chloe in the side of the neck first. She gasps as I pump her full of the liquid.

"What was that?" she asks.

"It disarms the bomb."

"Wait, really?"

I nod. Tommy tosses me a syringe from up front. I use it to inject Exodus.

Raphael glances back at me, "What happened in there?"

"I slit Mills' throat."

Dante injects Cass with his good hand, then Kennedy.

"Where are we going now?" Chloe asks Tommy.

"Lazarus has always had a backup plan, and so that's where we're heading."

He spins the wheel, turning the van down an empty street before handing Raphael a syringe.

Cass looks at Dante, "You're the Reaper who saved us?"

He nods, "Yeah."

"Thank you."

I gaze at Chloe, "So other than ripped clothes, are you okay?"

"Yeah, I'm good. You?"

"Other than a pounding heart, yeah."

She laces her fingers between mine.

Exodus smooths a hand through his white hair, "Guys, I'm freaking out."

"Why?" Kennedy asks.

"Well, gee, I wonder why? Maybe because we just escaped the Estate and now a bunch of Reapers are tracking us down?"

Kennedy rolls his eyes, "You lived in Salem for over five years, and yet you're scared of a few Reapers?"

"Shut up, Kennedy."

Tommy hits the breaks, "Alright, everyone, get out."

CHAPTER THIRTY-SEVEN

W e follow Tommy to the side of a tall brick building. He stops in front of a ladder, and climbs up. His backpack sways back and forth as he gains altitude.

Chloe follows after him. I tail the rest up the ladder. The climb takes roughly a minute. The wind whips my dirty blonde hair around when I make it to the top.

"Nice view," Chloe says. Looking over Seattle, the skyline is drowned in smog. Smoke rises from the factories to the north.

Raphael faces Tommy, "What are we doing here, Price?"

He points to an abandoned building near the Space Needle. Yellow warning tape surrounds the building and the neon ends sway in the chill breeze, "That's where we need to be."

"Then why are we up here?" I ask.

Dante points to the steel cable attached to one of the satellites on the roof. I follow the length and see that it ends in the city streets below, "Zipline. The Reapers are going to be looking for the van, so we had to ditch it to ensure that they won't be able to follow us."

Tommy nods, taking off his backpack, unzipping it, and pulling out a leather belt for each of us, "He's right. Each of you take a belt, wrap it around the cable, and step off the ledge."

"We know how ziplines work," Cass says, grabbing one of the belts and wrapping it around the cable. She glances over at Raphael, "See you on the other side."

She walks off the roof.

We watch her zip through the air, listening to the cable screech. Exodus grabs the next belt, followed by Kennedy, Raphael, and then Dante. Tommy and I take extra precautions to make sure he doesn't fall to his death.

I face Tommy, "You just keep on saving my life, man."

"It's a life worth saving," he remarks, handing me a belt. "I've known you since you were just a kid, and you'll always be like a little brother to me, Jay."

"Do you remember Julie?"

"Yeah, how could I forget a sassy blonde such as herself?"

"Dante said she was killed."

"I know. He was one of the Reapers who stormed the base in Jersey when Bleach was murdered. Everyone was dying, and I knew it was only a matter of time before I was found. I was right. He located me, but instead of putting one in between my eyes, he took his mask off and told me how he wanted revenge. I was shocked, and he told me to meet him at a certain café here in Seattle. That's when he shot the wall next to me, and I mimicked the sweet look of death," he stops for a moment. "You'd all be dead if it weren't for him."

"I know, I'll have to the thank him later."

He steps forward and places his belt around the rusted cable, "Yeah, if he lives through tonight"

"He's tough."

"Everybody's tough until they get their hand blown off."

He approaches the edge of the roof, and my ears burst, causing me to flinch back.

The cable tumbles to the earth below.

Tommy's eyes widen, "What? How did—"

Out of the corner of my eye, I see movement on the rooftop to our right. I lunge at Tommy and take him to the ground as a shot is fired. The bullet zooms past our collapsed bodies and slams into the vent at our side.

Tommy pulls out a handgun and fires at our assailant. I pull him to his feet.

"The ladder!" he shouts.

A Reaper finishing his ascent steps onto the roof and aims his gun directly at Tommy's forehead.

With one swift movement, I pull my pistol out of my back pocket and fire. The bullet hits him in his chest, but his armor absorbs the blast, knocking him off balance.

The sniper on the opposite roof fires another round as I charge the man in front of me. The bullet misses, barely.

I throw a fist into the Reaper's gasmask, hurting me more than it hurts him. He headbutts me, and I jolt back, grabbing his wrist. I turn his body to the side, and yank upward, ripping his arm out of the socket.

Metallic screams echo off the buildings. I feel a raindrop splash against my face.

He breaks free from my grip, ditching the handgun and pulling out a knife. He swings at me twice, but I reel back each time, countering with brutal kicks to the body.

His blade slashes down my face. It feels like it is on fire. A bitter sting sings with the hellish symphony.

My lips part. He pulls his arm back to thrust, but four bullets enter the side of his face, and he trips over the edge of the rooftop before plummeting into the roof of a vacant vehicle down below.

Blood torrents down my left cheek.

"Drop!" Tommy yells. A bullet hits the ground behind me, sending chunks of debris into the air.

More rain begins to fall.

Tommy aims at the sniper and fires, this time getting a lucky shot and lethally catching the assailant. He then pulls me to my feet. My cheek is surging with blood, staining my already ruined dress shirt.

"We need to go now," he says, and he descends the ladder.

I follow him and with each step, my cheek throbs harder. By the time our feet are touching the bottom, I feel lightheaded.

It's pouring now. The rain sprays the streets, our visibility growing weaker.

"Where to now?" I ask, following Tommy as he turns down an alley.

"We need to get to the others," he replies, picking up his pace.

The alleyway is similar to one I saw in the hallucination I had inside the Estate. The walls are littered with graffiti, the asphalt is flooded, and there's a disconcerting vibe in the air.

"Move your feet, Jay," his voice is muffled by the rain.

I stare at the black tags consisting of names, symbols, and phrases.

I can make out that one says, *"Long Live Lazarus."*

Gunfire erupts at the end of the alley. I drop back, my spine jolting as I hit the ground. I aim and fire, catching one of the Reapers in the neck. He crashes to the floor, and his buddy aims at me, but I'm quicker and put one in his tinted eyes.

I take a deep breath, quickly getting to my feet, "These pricks won't stop coming!"

Tommy doesn't reply. He stands still with his back to me.

"Tommy? You good?"

No reply.

I step up to him. My heart is pounding inside my throat.

A mangled mess is all that is left of his throat. Multiple bullet holes etch his flesh. Blood is spurting from the wounds. He stares at me with bulging eyes, grasping his throat. His bottom lip is shaking.

He falls into me, and I attempt to keep him steady.

The world goes still.

I can't hear the rain.

"Fine," he gargles, his words come out with a mouthful of scarlet. "Jay, I'm fine."

"No," I sound faint. My eyes are misty with red. "No, no don't do this to me."

He stares wide and desperate. He tries to say something, but slumps even further, falling to the street.

A noisy hum of an engine approaches the alley, but my reflexes don't kick in. I can only stare at my lifeless friend while bloody rain puddles form around his face.

Chloe's voice fills the inside my head.

Run.

I sprint away. Weak sobs escape from my lips as multiple Reapers storm the alley.

I leave his body behind in the freezing wet detachment of the night.

CHAPTER THIRTY-EIGHT

Exodus' shoulders go lax when he sees me sprinting toward him and the others, "Jason?"

I don't reply.

Dante tilts his head, "Where's Price?"

Kennedy shoots me a bewildered look, "What happened to your face."

I skid to a stop in front of them all, my chest heaving up and down, blood streaming from my eyes, "We need to get to that building. *Now.*"

Chloe stares at me, "Jason, where's Tommy?"

I stare at her, lighting cracking overhead, "Dead."

⁂

THE INSIDE OF THE OLD ABANDONED BUILDING IS dimly lit. The concrete floor and cracked walls suit the stale and foul-smelling air.

"Why are we here?" Raphael asks.

"There's an elevator up ahead. Get in, and then you'll see

why," Dante replies. He's pale from the loss of blood. His brown eyes grow darker.

We follow him down another corridor, and at the end of the hall is an elevator with grey doors. It looks in disrepair, and my stomach roils at the thought of being trapped inside. None of that really matters though, does it?

Tommy is dead. . . he's actually dead.

Exodus presses the call button on the elevator, and a few moments later, the doors part and the seven of us enter. The metal box groans under our combined weight.

Dante presses a button, and the doors reunite.

Cass leans up against one side of the cab. Her blue eyes are misty with tears, "He's actually gone."

Kennedy folds his arms, "Which one? Sam? Ross? Tommy? We've lost so many people."

"All of them. It isn't fair."

Raphael looks at her, "Life isn't fair, and it never will be."

Chloe shudders out a sigh, and her eyes fill with bloody tears, "Can you three just shut up?"

A sick sounding *ding* breaks our dissolution, and the elevator comes to a halt. The doors part once again. I'm surprised by the sizeable assembly of Lazarus members standing in the lobby. Each one is armed, wearing the signature uniform, including black morph masks. My strange symbol is pressed to the upper chest of each member. The slanted eyes scrutinize me.

I glance at Dante, "I thought all of Lazarus was wiped out?"

"You thought wrong," he replies. His frame trembles. "These members served as moles for years, and each of them are military trained. All are ready to help us overthrow Mills and wipe out the God Code."

Dante abruptly collapses to the floor, and two members rush to help him to his feet.

A third member – one without a mask on – looks at us, "My

name's Lucas; I'm one of the medics, so any of you who're injured can come with me to receive medical attention."

I step forward, "That'll just be me and Dante."

He nods, and I follow the two members as they carry Julie's father out of the assemblage. Lucas escorts us down numerous hallways. Each one in desperate need of cleaning and repair. The lights above flicker, the walls are painted with stains, and the floors are tarnished with various liquids.

"What is this place anyway?" I ask Lucas, my steps slowing. The gash on my face is still bleeding.

"It *was* a factory, but now it's our base of operations," he replies, opening a metal door. "It was closed last year for being a safety risk, but there aren't any plans on tearing it down or even remodeling. We figured that it was the last place Mills and his military would look."

I enter the room, relieved to see that it's some type of infirmary. Four hospital beds are placed in the center, there's a bathroom to the left. A few carts are spaced throughout with all different kinds of syringes, surgical tools, and much more.

I drag my feet across the white marble floor to one of the beds, "Will my friend be okay?"

"I'm sure. Whoever stopped the bleeding is a lifesaver."

I collapse on the bed. My blood smears the white pillow.

The two other Lazarus members quickly place Dante on a bed and resituate my body so that it's not falling off the sheet and onto the floor.

Lucas walks to me with a syringe in his hand, "I'm going to put you under for a bit, okay?"

"I just need some stitches. No need."

"Trust me, with a gash that big, you're gonna want to be asleep."

"Could you also check my hands and feet?"

"Why?"

"No nails."

"What?"

"Just check them."

"I will. I'm going to dope you up first."

He inserts the needle into a vein. I can feel the warm liquid entering my bloodstream. For the next couple of seconds, I glance around the room until the corners of my vision turn black and dull reality.

CHAPTER THIRTY-NINE

A cool night breeze flows through my hair. I watch the fireworks ignite in the sky, while Simon holds a bottle of whiskey out for me.

"You sure you don't want some?" he asks, his dress shirt untucked and his tie loose around his neck.

"I'll pass."

"*Boooo.*"

A little chuckle escapes my mouth as another firework goes off, "We still have school tomorrow, and I don't wanna wake up feeling like a zombie, douche-face."

"Fine, whatever," he brings the bottle up to his lips before taking a swig.

We're on the roof of one of the local stores just outside of Brookhaven, watching the firework display that the government puts on every year to celebrate President Mills' birthday, November 13th. It's the only night of the year where we're allowed to stay out past curfew. There are parades in the street, a festival downtown, and not a care in the world.

"Where's Julie?" I ask, grabbing a handful of potato chips from a bag we bought earlier today. "She said she would meet us here."

A voice from behind us says, "Oh, I've been here for a while."

The two of us recoil. I turn to see Julie standing a couple of feet behind us, "Are you *trying* to make us crap our pants?"

"Gross," she says, stepping forward before sitting down in between me and Simon.

Simon puts his arm around her, "You want a sip?"

"Not really, no."

"You and Jason are a bunch of pansies."

"Whatever, fireball breath."

Another firework goes off, painting the sky different shades of red, white, and blue.

Julie turns to me, "You feeling better?"

My shoulders fall a bit, "I guess."

Simon takes another swig, "You need to tell Tommy."

"You know I can't do that," I say. "Jakob already makes my life hell, so why would I make it worse by telling a Saint?"

"Because he'll do something about it."

"Sure, whatever."

"Fifi deserves better than what happened to her. Don't you want to get revenge?"

I sigh, "Revenge is a fool's game."

"Only people who haven't had revenge say that," Simon retorts.

Julie grabs a handful of chips, "I'm with Simon on this one."

I gradually get to my feet, "And what if Tommy does nothing, huh? Then Jakob is going to literally kill me, and I don't know about you two, but that would suck."

"Do your parents know?" Simon asks.

"No, they think she was just hit by a car."

Julie's eyes widen, "Is that how bad Jakob beat her?"

My chest burns, and I snatch the whiskey bottle out of Simon's hand, downing a mouthful. It hurts my throat as I swallow, but I don't care. I need a distraction.

I loved the way that Fifi would always hop up into my bed when it was raining.

Fire rushes through my veins, and I stand.

"Dude!" Simon blurts and I chuck the bottle down to the streets below.

It shatters, and tears begin to spill down my cheeks, "I hate him. I hate him *so* much."

Julie slowly gets to her feet and hugs me, "It's okay. He'll get what's coming to him, I promise."

"I was taking her on a walk, and he and Eli just came out of nowhere and started kicking her."

Simon gets to his feet as well, walking over and putting an arm around me, "I know, man, I know. Just think, next year we'll be graduated and you won't have to deal with that fat-faced dick ever again."

I nod, my bottom lip quivering, "Yeah, I know."

"Until then," Julie says, shooting me a half smile. "The three of us will stick together, like always."

Another firework explodes in the sky. My heart still aches, but I reply, "Okay."

Simon steps over to his grocery bag and pulls out another bottle of whiskey, "Luckily, I took the liberty of buying two."

"You know, one day they're gonna find out about the fake ID," Julie flashes him an unamused look.

"I didn't even have to use it," he remarks, a superior grin on his face. "James was working."

She rolls her eyes, "Of course he was."

I chuckle, wiping my flushed cheeks before taking a deep breath, "Let's go get a doughnut or something."

"Good idea," Simon agrees.

Julie shrugs, "Sure, just as long as I'm not paying."

"I don't have any money," I say.

Simon pulls some cash out of his front pocket, "Don't worry, I took some money from my mom's purse."

Julie shakes her head, suppressing her giggle, "And you wonder why she hates you so much."

"Eh, who cares."

The three of us chuckle.

><

MY EYES SHOOT OPEN. ALL PAIN THAT ONCE RESTRICTED me is now gone. I'm in the Lazarus uniform, and the gash around my face is numb, but the skin around it feels tight.

"You've been stitched up," Lucas said. He puts something down on one of the carts. "I also went ahead and cleaned your fingertips and toes."

I lift my hands up to my face, but they're both covered by a glove, "Will I need to wear these?"

"Yes, unless you have a major fetish for infections and maybe even missing fingers."

I sit up and search for Dante. He's also wearing the Lazarus uniform, and a metal hook is where his hand used to be.

"A hook?" I question, refraining from sounding sarcastic.

"It's just until we can get him a prosthetic."

I step off of the bed. My head spins as a result of the swift dismount. After I steady myself, I glance over at Lucas and ask if I can leave. He tells me that I can, so I sluggishly walk to the door. The bright lights above cause my eyes to strain.

"He's awake," Chloe sighs. She's sitting in the hall with Raphael and Exodus.

"How long have you been waiting?" I ask, smiling at the sight of them.

"Four hours," Raphael replies, stepping forward. "How's Dante?"

"He'll be fine."

Chloe wraps her arms around me, "How do you feel?"

"Dazed, honestly. I never thought we were going to escape the Estate and make it here alive."

"Some of us didn't," Raphael states.

Exodus sighs, "Way to be a downer, man."

"It's true," he says, a cold look appearing in his eyes. "We're going to go look for Tommy's body in the morning. I just hope the Reapers didn't take it."

"Me too," I say. "Where are we sleeping? I just need to lie down."

Exodus nods, "Not a bad idea. follow us."

Chloe places her fingers in between mine, and the four of us make our way down the hall. We walk into a cramped room with sleeping bags on the floor. Kennedy and Cass are sound asleep.

I claim a sleeping bag, propping a pillow up against the wall and leaning against it. Chloe takes the one next to me, and both Raphael and Exodus find a couple close by. Despite being in a dark room, lying on the frigid concrete floor, and having a stitched-up face, I feel comfortable.

Anything beats being a slave to the President.

After some moments of silence, Chloe scooches closer to me, placing her hand on my chest, "I'm sorry that you had to watch him die."

I stare at her a moment, "I've known him for so long."

"I know."

I place my hand on the side of her face, and she leans in, kissing me.

Exodus groans, "It's kinda hard to sleep over the sound of tongue wrestling, dudes."

Chloe and I part, snickering.

Raphael repositions himself, "Remember when we first met, Frye?"

"Yeah, how could I forget? I stabbed you in the throat."

"Ah, weren't those the days? No impending doom of a biochemical weapon, our friends were alive, hope was abundant."

Exodus turns to face the wall, "Like I said, way to be a downer."

"We're going to destroy the God Code," Chloe says. "And after that, we're going to let everyone in the nation know Mills' plans – that'll certainly be the cause of absolute chaos."

"And then what?" I ask.

"I don't know."

"Kill Mills, then take out the rest of the government before rebuilding America," Raphael says.

Chloe stares up at the ceiling, "It seems like there are so many loose ends that we need to clean up before we can start *rebuilding*."

"Of course, but won't it be worth it? That's the point of Lazarus; that's why we're here."

I sit up a bit, "Exactly."

Kennedy tosses in his sleeping bag, "Trying to sleep here."

"And?" Raphael pops his neck, causing his jet-black hair to flop over his head.

Cass sighs, "I'm trying to sleep, too."

Chloe sits up, and to my surprise, she gets out of her sleeping bag and on her feet.

"Where are you going?" I ask.

The air smells as stale as ever.

"I need to clear my mind."

"Want me to come with?"

"Sure."

Her expression is hard to read. It makes my stomach twist.

I get out of my bag and follow her to the door. We step out into the corridor.

"I heard pregnancy sucks!" Exodus call out after us.

"Shut up, Blaine," Raphael demands.

The door shuts behind us, and we make our way down the hall, our shoes plodding against the white marble.

"Are you okay?" I ask, my arms hanging at my sides.

She chews her bottom lip, "I don't think so."

"Did I do something wrong?"

She chuckles, "No."

"Then what? You look like you're about to cry."

"The only thing that's going to make me cry is you telling me that I look like I'm about to cry."

"My bad."

She takes a long exhale, "During the two-week torture session, they didn't physically harm me; just injected me with this hallucinatory drug that made me see awful things, just like I told you."

"Yeah?"

"I lied to you."

"Huh?"

"Back when we first met, I lied to you."

"About what?"

"My dad's car accident."

"Oh. . .?"

We stop walking, "My dad liked to gamble, and he was good at it. But one day, he lost to the wrong guy, and we were in serious debt," she kicks a stray pebble down the hall. "He started to do terrible things for money. He hurt people, robbed them, left them in a heaping mess. . . My mom didn't catch on, but I knew. I couldn't help eavesdropping in on his phone calls," she rubs her eyes, traces of blood appearing. "He eventually paid the guy back, but all the stuff he had to do for the money left him in a twisted shell of his former self. He turned to heavy drugs and alcohol, and one night, he lost it."

"You don't have tell me all this," I quietly respond.

"I want to."

"Are you sure?"

She nods.

"Then go ahead."

"Like I said, one night he lost it. Our next door neighbor happened to have a daughter who was my best friend, and she had a little chihuahua that wouldn't shut up. I guess my dad couldn't take it. He hopped the fence and snapped the poor dog's neck. His mind was fried from all the crap he was taking. The only reason I know this is because I ran after him after he left the house in his drunken rage," she stops, glancing up at the ceiling. "My friend came out, mortified at what she saw. My dad was holding her dog by the throat. She screamed, and he went after her," she stops again, unable to hold in her tears any longer. "He was sick. . . not himself. He didn't know what he was doing, and I did nothing to stop him."

She lets herself fall into my arms.

"He sobered up after, but just couldn't cope with what he did. He killed himself, and it's all my fault."

I'm at a loss for words, "Ch-Chloe."

She looks up, "My family moved to Collingsworth after that, and my mom had to make ends meet any way she could. I ran away, got mixed in with bad people, but eventually went home and started helping out. That's when we were all killed."

I softly scratch her back, my heart aching for her, "I don't even know what to say."

"I know this is all coming out of nowhere, but those hallucinations. . . they were all of my dad, and I just needed to talk to someone about it."

I kiss her forehead, "I'm glad I was that someone."

"I wouldn't want anyone else to be my someone."

My chest bursts with warmth, and I hold onto her tighter, never wanting to let go.

I'd be dead without her.

CHAPTER FORTY

TWO MONTHS LATER...

We never found Tommy's body. We searched and searched, but no body, not even a trail of blood.

These last two months have been filled with training and planning. Tomorrow is Christmas Eve. What if we can't shut down the God Code? Everyone will die the same way Bleach did, and the world will start over again. We will be lost and forgotten.

I throw my palm into the punching bag and swiftly turn, swinging a kick. Each strike connects, making my red target sway violently from side to side.

I'm on the diet and exercise plan Tommy had me on back in New Jersey. The results are phenomenal. I've surpassed my Fight-Night build. I'm physically ready for anything tonight has in store for me. My fingernails have practically grown back, my wounds have healed, and I feel strong.

We have scouts stalking the woods surrounding the facility. They scope out our target and find the best way to attack. Raphael and Dante have been up day and night planning, and the others have been training nonstop.

"Hey," Chloe enters the makeshift gym in her Lazarus uniform. "Raph says that it's time for our final briefing."

I swing a fist into the bag, "Right now?"

"Yeah, we're just waiting on you."

I stop my target from swaying, "Alright, I'll be there in a second."

She steps a bit further into the gym, "We're going to win tonight, I can feel it."

"I keep having doubts."

"Why? If we fail, everyone dies."

"I know. You're right. . . we can't fail, we just can't."

She tosses me the Lazarus hoodie, and I put it on, sweat pouring down my frame. She hands me a pair of pants, and after I slide them up my scarred legs, she glances at my chest.

"What is it?" I ask.

She's quiet for a moment, and musty air fills my lungs, "The symbol. How did you come up with it?"

I glance down at the crude scowl with two creature-like eyes slanted in rage, "That night was. . . something I'll never forget. All the pain, rage, and inhumanity. The symbol was a statement of uprising, a promise to overthrow and restart. It takes a monster to kill a monster, and that's what we are – a bunch of monsters who sacrifice pieces of themselves to save others," I pause before taking off my gloves and tossing them to the floor. "But you know what? The only thing I regret from that evening was bringing Matthew back to life. If I never did that, then Simon would still be alive and here with us right now."

"I'm sorry, I shouldn't have asked."

"No, it's fine. Let's get to the briefing."

"Okay, lead the way."

I nod, stepping away from the punching bag and leaving the gym. Chloe follows me down multiple hallways, up a stairwell, and down another hall before stopping in front of a door with a stenciled sign.

Chloe grabs my hand, our fingers laced together.

"What happens next?" I ask

She turns and faces me, her grip cold, "It's like what Raph said; we go after Mills, kill him, and take America back before rebuilding it."

I sigh, "That sounds like some optimistic bullcrap."

"What do you mean?"

"It's not that easy, and you know it. There's only two hundred of us. Mills has millions, not to mention that the population doesn't exactly like us."

"We'll get them to like us. We'll show them the truth about tonight; how Mills planned on killing them all, and how we stopped him."

"You always know what to say, don't you?"

We stare at each other. Her eyes are so pretty, yet intimidating. I feel like she has the ability to see right through me and discover my real thoughts. And the real thoughts swimming around my head right now are that we could potentially fail and all die tonight.

CHAPTER FORTY-ONE

"Team A, you'll be ambushing from this side," Dante points to the left side of the map showing an aerial view of the God Code facility. He slides his index over to the right side, "And team B, you'll be ambushing from this side."

Raphael points to the wooded area that faces the front of the facility. The large gate stands out, "Team C, you'll quietly take out the Saints who're guarding the blockade. After that, you'll hack the gate and get it to retract back into the ground."

"And after that," Dante starts, his jet-black metal hook points, "We send in our special surprise and then open fire. We have some of the scouts mapping out the area as we speak. Once they return, we'll know exactly what we're up against."

Lucas raises his hand, "Are you going to tell us about the helmets you made us?"

Raphael shakes his head, "They aren't helmets," He slides his index finger across the large screen, switching the image to a set of blueprints. "As you all can see, they resemble Vice's mask almost entirely. Underneath the metallic exterior, there's advanced Kevlar. These babies are kind of bullet resistant. Small calipers aren't much of a problem. Well, actually, it would be hellish, and there's a major chance you'll black out with brain hemorrhaging, but it beats getting the contents of your skull sprayed out everywhere. Just don't be stupid and get shot in the head, alright?"

Lars, one of the other medics, raises his hand, "I know we talked about this last briefing, but tell me again how we're going to shut this baby down?"

Raphael leans up against the wall with his arms folded as Dante slides his finger across the screen once more, revealing a high-quality image of the God Code, "One of our scouts were able to get a device inside a vent, and it captured this video."

Dante double taps the large screen, and the video begins. Two men stand next to the biochemical weapon, and I immediately recognize one of them as the man who showed me what was left of Bleach. I attempt to blot out the memory of her rotting flesh, missing teeth and eyes, and her shedding hair.

"You can't tell anyone about this," he tells his companion. The facility appears empty besides those two. "If you do, we'll both be killed, and you don't want that."

The other scientist sighs, "Why would I tell anyone? Installing the kill switch was the best decision we could've made. Now Mills will have to let us live with his other select few."

"And if he doesn't, then we'll activate the kill switch and tell the world everything."

"Good thinking, sir."

The video cuts, and Raphael speaks up, "The kill switch they're referring to is located on the left side of the device, and is labeled with the numbers 383829. We press it, and we can only assume that it'll destroy the weapon and prevent the disease inside from spreading."

Dante presses on the screen a few times, shutting it off, "Mills had a wireless remote that could set it off with the touch of a button. I stole it, but gave it to Thomas Price before his death. So we'll have to trust that the kill switch will work."

The door to the room opens, and everyone's head swivels to the right. Standing in the doorway is a scout named Jackal. He tosses Raph a set of keys.

"Updates?" Dante asks.

He nods, "Five truckloads of Reapers and Saints just arrived at the facility, including Matthew White."

I abruptly stand from my seat, "What's that piss-wad doing there?"

He shrugs, "Hell if I know, sir. The Reapers and Saints are scattered throughout the perimeter, and there's a squad of snipers up on the roof."

Raphael grunts, "Makes sense that they would take drastic measures. They know we're coming."

Chloe stands from her seat next to me, approaching Raphael and whispering something into his ear. He nods, and she returns, pulling her hair up in a ponytail.

"I almost forgot," Raphael starts, his posture straight, his eyes dark and cunning. "For those driving the suicide trucks, don't forget the two switches you have to flip in order to unlock the door. Once you make it inside the perimeter, you'll have six seconds to get out before it blows."

We all nod.

Dante glances out the window at the setting sun, "You all have twenty minutes to get geared up. Once you're done getting dressed, head to the back where all of the pickups are."

"And don't forget the plan," Raphael orders.

We all stand, my thoughts feel corrupted with thoughts of revenge.

Matthew was never supposed to be there, and the fact that he is fills me with both rage and excitement.

That piss-face will regret what he did to me and my family.

CHAPTER FORTY-TWO

I stare at myself in the bathroom mirror. The gash down my face has scarred, and the area around it is no longer broken and bruised from my prolonged torture session inside of the Estate.

I wear a tight black thermal shirt with Kevlar padding underneath. My dark blue jeans are also padded with Kevlar. I've got on knee pads and tactical gloves. There's a holster attached to my thigh with a handgun inside.

I put on my mask. Surprisingly, it's easy to breathe in, and fits like a second skin. I look like an inky black shadow. You can't see any facial features. With all of my other gear on, I'm unrecognizable.

The bathroom door opens to Raphael, who's all geared up minus his mask. He approaches the mirror and stops next to me. He has a combat knife in his grip.

"You ready?" he asks.

"Yeah, you?"

"As ready as I'll ever be," he pauses for a moment. "You have to stay focused tonight. I know White's there, but you have to put your vendetta aside and shut the God Code down first."

"I know," I grab a similar knife off the counter and loop it through my belt. "Are all the guns out back?"

"Yeah."

"Raph, if we fail—"

"We're not."

"I guess I'm just trying to come to terms."

"Come to terms with what?"

"That I might die tonight."

He stares at himself in the mirror, "Don't let it fog your mind, Pinder. The last thing I want is for you to get murked because your fear made you hesitate."

"Tonight feels bleak, man. There's two hundred and eighty-seven of us, and who knows how many of them. If we fail, everyone will die, and everything we've ever done won't matter."

"When I was sixteen, Vice sent me on a suicide mission to prove that I was worthy of being his heir. There were two ex-Lazarus members who were going to rat us out, and I had to kill both of them before they could talk. These two had a rap sheet of over a hundred confirmed kills each, and I was to do this alone."

"What happened?"

"I'm still here, aren't I? Point is, everyone told me that I wasn't going to make it, and how Vice was an idiot for thinking that I was even capable of being his successor. It was bleak, Jason, but there's one thing I've learned from my many years here at Lazarus."

"Which is?"

"You can't kill death. . . and we, Pinder, are death."

"What do you mean?"

"Lazarus isn't just an organization, it's an ideology, and no matter how hard anyone tries, you can't erase the thoughts of many. We are unavoidable, just like death."

I look at myself, his words sparking my adrenaline, "Just like death."

CHAPTER FORTY-THREE

"Is the checkpoint on the west side clear?" Raphael asks.

A voice comes back through the radio, "Yes, the two Saints are KIA and the cameras have been destroyed."

"Good, we're approaching."

"Got it."

It's pitch-black out. I wish the moonlight illuminated our path more. My window is rolled down, and the cool breeze flutters through the pickup's interior. The frigid winter air keeps me focused.

Chloe's with a different squad. I don't like it.

We have eight members in the bed of the truck. They are all armed to the teeth and have their heads down. Twenty other pickups tail us. Our convoy is not drawing any attention. We have members that simultaneously took out each individual checkpoint around Seattle. Military presence in this city has grown thin, and it's going to keep thinning and thinning until there's no one left to stand against us.

Raphael slowly brakes as a checkpoint comes into view. Two Lazarus members approach our vehicle and hop into the back seats. After they shut their doors, we speed toward Seattle's outskirts. My heart pounds.

After a bit of silence, Raphael glances over at me, "Tell team A to take a left up ahead at the fork."

I nod, unclipping my walkie talkie from my uniform and holding the button down, "Team A, take a left at the fork."

A second later, someone shoots back, "Got it. Taking a left at the fork."

We continue straight, but the last eight vehicles in the convoy take a left.

"Team B needs to take a right up here in a minute," Raphael says.

Again, I nod, bringing the walkie talkie up to my lips, "Team B, take a right up ahead."

"Yes, sir."

Like last time, we continue straight, but Team B takes a right, leaving us with only five pickups.

The forest around us is thick and tall, and the path ahead of us is barely visible since we aren't using any headlights. It isn't until Raphael hits the brakes and turns off into some brush when I know we're close to our target.

The large gate guarding the God Code facility is about a mile ahead. From memory, I note how two Saints stand guard out front, armed with assault rifles and body armor.

Raphael turns to me, shutting the truck off, "Take Jackal and go kill the Saints out front. We'll be right behind you."

I nod, stepping out of the pickup and tapping the side of the vehicle, "Jackal, let's go."

"Yes, sir," he jumps out of the bed and unsheathes his knife. "We shouldn't use guns unless we have to."

I nod, leaning my assault rifle against the passenger side door before pulling out my knife and gripping it in my left hand, "Alright, lead the way."

The two of us sprint toward our targets, keeping our steps

silent. I take the left side of the path, and he takes the right, using the tall grass and trees to our advantage. For about six minutes, we run until we reach our destination. The gate is only twenty feet ahead, and four guards are standing at attention.

Jackal turns to face me, "I'll create a distraction, hang back."

"Got it."

He creeps ahead like a predator, crouched down and using the nature around him as cover. He gets closer and closer, and eventually, he picks something up off the ground and chucks it into the trees near the gate.

The Saints look toward the disturbance, and one of them leaves his position to investigate, but the one on the far right speaks up, "Don't leave your post. They're here."

He glances back, "But what if—"

"Shut the hell up and stay vigilant."

They aren't biting.

I put my knife away and exchange it for my handgun, switching it off safety. Putting one foot in front of the other, I creep down the path, keeping my body hidden by the trees. My dark clothes give me the upper hand. I get closer, and when I'm about five feet away, I aim my gun up at one of them.

When I pull this trigger, it'll be nonstop carnage until one side is completely killed off.

My heart beats out of my chest, and my stomach churns with anxiety.

My finger is tense on the trigger, but I don't squeeze. Not yet.

I'm scared.

Jackal lunges out from the brush and thrusts his knife into one of the Saints' neck. The three others attempt to put him down, but I open fire, emptying my magazine on them.

Jackal throws his victim to the ground, glancing at me as the soldier chokes, "Get over here, and hurry."

I sprint to his side.

He pulls out a device and sticks it to the gate, holding his index finger up at me, "Give it a second."

A moment later, the small metal contraption chimes, and the gate retracts into the ground, rumbling the earth below my feet. I watch the pebbles in the path tremble.

Jackal sprints behind some cover, but a shot is fired, and I flinch as his head bursts into a bloody mess. A splintered piece of his skull hits my mask.

I dive to the side as another shot is fired. This bullet penetrates the dirt next to me.

I hastily grab my walkie talkie and put it up to my lips, "Send in the truck! Do it *now!*"

"On it!" Someone replies.

More gunshots fly through the air, assuring me that Team A and B both accomplished their assignments.

I glance at Jackal on the ground, the upper part of his skull and the mask that covered it are both gone with blood, bone fragments, and brain splattered all around him.

The snipers on the roof killed him.

The approaching sound of a speeding vehicle causes me to look back. One of the red pickups speeds down the trail. Its headlights are on, and c4 is attached to all sides. It zooms past me, and I watch as the truck is littered with bullets, the windshield is shattered, and the driver is presumably killed.

It nears the front of the facility.

"*Now!*" I blurt into the radio, and a second later, the truck explodes into a fireball, killing the twenty-something Reapers and canines at the front entrance. It also blasts the front doors open.

Another truck comes speeding down the trail; both sides are covered in heavy steel plates, the windshield and windows have thick material coated against it – all meant to stop bullets. It screeches to a halt in front of me, and a handful of members hop out of the bed on the left side.

I join them.

"Keep your heads down," I say as a bullet slams into the side of the truck.

One of the members nudges me "You think we'll make it through tonight, boss?"

Another bullet hits the truck, but it does nothing, "Of course we are."

The truck moves forward. The makeshift cover takes countless numbers of bullets. Eventually one of the windows shatters, and the member who was just talking to me takes a bullet to the back of the mask.

He lurches forward, "*Shi—*"

One the snipers on the roof gets a clear shot and sends a bullet through his face.

"I said lower your heads!" I blurt, another bullet zooming through the same window.

They do as they're told, and I look ahead to see Team A moving forward behind another armored truck, numerous shots being fired at them as well.

"Kill them all!" a metallic voice orders from up ahead.

My eyes widen as a concourse of bullets begin to rip our truck apart; every window shatters, two tires are shredded, and another member by my side takes three bullets to the neck.

The truck stops, and the driver door slowly opens. The man behind the wheel steps out, blood oozing from the wounds in his body. He begins stumbling away.

One of the other guys in my squad looks over at him, "*No! No, Lucas!*"

I watch with wide eyes as the medic collapses on the grass.

A member from Team A looks over at us, "Enemy to your left!"

The second my mind comprehends his words, a Reaper steps out from the front of the truck and guns down the man ahead of me, one of the bullets going through his neck and hitting me in the gut. My Kevlar shields me from too much damage, but the air escapes from my lungs nonetheless.

I fall to my knees, and the Reaper aims his weapon down at my head.

He gets the back of his skull split open by oncoming fire sent out by Team A.

A member standing a few feet back runs up and pulls me to my feet. My lungs still refuse to cooperate. Some of my ribs are broken, and the pounding from my heart doesn't help.

"We've got to get inside the facility!" he yells, another group of bullets hitting our motionless cover.

I nod, sluggishly pointing over to the driver's seat, "Get in, and step on it. Keep your head low, and bail out before you hit the front doors."

"But sir—"

"Just do it."

He reluctantly moves to the opened door and hops in, slouching down as far as he can.

I jump into the bed of the truck, and the surviving members next to me do the same, both hopping in and keeping their heads low.

A moment later, the truck lurches forward, speeding through a crowd of soldiers, running them down and crushing their bodies beneath the wheels.

One of the snipers on the roof fires a round, and the bullet zooms past my face.

The member next to me screams, grasping his bloodied shoulder, splintered bone sticking out of his shirt, "I'm hit! I'm hit!"

I stare at the blood gushing out of his wound, "You're going to be okay!"

The second Lazarus member in the bed takes a bullet to his face, courtesy of the snipers above. I look away to avoid seeing the carnage.

"I—" the wounded member by my side blurts. "I don't want to die!"

The driver door to the pickup flies open, and the man driving bails out, rolling through the grass as his body hits the ground.

I peer over the side of the still speeding vehicle, seeing that we're about to crash into the five Reapers guarding the door-less entrance.

Get the hell out of the truck, you idiot!

I look over at the screaming Lazarus member, my guilt eating me alive.

I can't just leave him.

Before I get to argue with myself more, the truck rams into the entrance, stopping as the roof of the vehicle slams into the doorway.

Crap!

I go limp, acting dead as multiple sets of feet rush toward the truck.

"I don't wanna die!" the member screams.

Five Reapers appear on either side of the bed, aim at the wounded man, and shoot.

The gunfire bursts through my eardrums, sending an unbearable ring to bounce around my head.

A storm of bullets rip the Reapers apart, and I jolt up, seeing one of Team B's trucks speeding toward the facility, seven members in the bed are shooting every hostile they see.

One of the snipers up on the roof blast one of them in the head. I rapidly glance around at an army of Reapers marching out of the facility, but they can't see me.

I quickly jump out of the truck and sprint to the right side of the facility. The sound of gunshots mask my footing.

I stumble over a corpse, my mind recalling how one of our scouts was able to get a device into a large air duct that was easily accessible. It was on the right side of the facility, and I think I know where it is.

I turn and sprint down the side of the building. My adrenaline fuels my actions.

I constantly scan the wall with my eyes. It takes a moment before I can find it. I groan when I see that the vent is just out of reach.

That won't stop me, though.

"Who are you?"

I turn to see Chloe. Her mask isn't on, but she's unharmed.

"It's me, Jason. Why aren't you wearing your mask?'" I question, staring at her with wide eyes.

"It's too hard to breathe," she pauses, glancing over at the vent. "I'm guessing we came here for the same reasons?"

I nod, "I'll give you a boost."

"No, you go ahead. I've got your back."

I eject the empty magazine, put a fresh one in, then fire at the metal cover that blocks access to the duct.

I take a few steps back, breathe, and sprint forward, jumping up and catching the ledge. A sharp pain shoots through my chest, reminding me that I am injured.

I hoist myself up, "Go help where you can, and put the mask back on."

"I will."

I holster my gun, take a deep breath, then crawl through the freezing channel of airways.

It's extremely dark, but I remember the modifications that my mask includes. Reaching my hand up, I feel the back of my skin-tight disguise and hold my finger down on a small sensor.

Everything lights up as if it were day, and I grin, continuing my way through the vent.

I keep crawling until I see another vent cover. I peer down. The light from the room below blinds me.

I switch the night-vision off.

"Mr. White, I can't hear you!" a man inside the room practically yells. "There's gunshots going off at every second, and nothing you're saying makes sense."

Using the sound to my advantage, I grab the cover and begin to pry it open. It squeaks and groans, but it eventually tears off, and I set it down behind me.

"Please repeat yourself, sir!" the Saint yells.

I can't drop down, that would be too much noise, and he'd detect the vibration. So instead, I lower myself upside down, using my legs as support.

"You want *what?*" the Saint yells with his back turned to me. His body is within an arm's reach.

I unsheathe my knife, using my other hand to softly tap on the Saint's shoulder.

He flinches, quickly turning.

I abruptly slash his throat, watching with a cold stare as he collapses to the floor. The fight outside masks the sound of his gargling.

I drop down, landing on my feet. Grabbing the walkie talkie out of the dead man's grip, I throw it against the wall, smashing it.

Someone drops down behind me, and I thrust my knife at whoever it is.

"Chill out!" he blurts, and I see that it's one of my members.

"Who are you?" I ask.

"Exodus."

"Blaine?" I ask.

He nods.

"How did you find the vent?"

"I didn't always sleep during briefings."

"Well, what now?"

He looks down at the corpse on the floor, pausing for a moment, "We kill Matthew."

My eyes widen, a sinister grin appearing underneath the mask, "How?"

"I have an idea, but it's risky."

"I'll do anything, just as long as it won't get me killed."

He chuckles, "How ironic of you to say."

CHAPTER FORTY-FOUR

Exodus struggles to open the door with me in his arms. He's wearing the dead Saint's uniform, his ski mask caked with blood.

Eventually, he gets the door open, and the two of us exit. My right hand sways limply at my side.

The facility's interior is in shambles. The lights above flicker, numerous scientists hide under desks, and what's left of the military force is outside fighting a bloody battle.

Exodus approaches the stairs, and since nobody can see my face, I keep my eyes open.

"You sure there isn't an elevator?" he asks me as he begins his ascent up the staircase.

I shake my head ever so slightly.

It takes him four minutes to get to the fourth floor, and he carries me down the hall and to the right. I see Matthew's office door at the end of the corridor. Two Reapers stand guard.

"What's going on down there? Why isn't Lazarus dead yet?" one of them asks Exodus.

He shakes his head, "We're losing numbers rapidly, and I need to see Mr. White immediately."

"Why?" the other asks.

"This is Jason Pinder."

"Is he dead?"

"Yes, killed him myself."

The two guards exchange looks, and one of them turns and bangs on the door, "Sir, you need to see this."

Due to all the gunshots, it's almost inaudible to hear Matthew reply with, "The door's unlocked."

The Reaper opens the door, and Exodus enters.

My heart pounds, and it takes every ounce of energy I have not to breathe.

The Reapers enter behind us, and one of them shuts the door.

Matthew sits behind his desk. A gun rests on the surface. He looks up at us, his one eye filled with something I've never seen before.

Fear.

"What's going on down there? Nobody's answering me," he says.

Exodus drops my body down on the ground, "None of that matters now, sir."

"And why do you assume that?"

"Because the man I just brought in is Jason Pinder."

The fear leaves Matthew's eye, and in its place, mania, "Prove it!"

Exodus pulls the mask from my face. I close my eyes.

I hear Matthew stand, "It's him. I—It's really him!"

One of the Reapers speak up, "I wouldn't get too excited."

"Why not?"

"Tell him."

Exodus clears his throat, "They're killing us, sir."

"And we're killing them back, so what?"

"Yes, but we underestimated them. They're using car bombs, trucks with armor plating all over them, fully automatic weapons—"

"Get out of my office. All of you."

"But—"

"*Now!* Get out, *now!*"

The three of them don't argue, and I hear them walk away, shutting the door behind them.

Matthew carefully approaches me. I can hear his breath, and it's harsh and unsteady, "I should've been the one to kill you, but that idiotic old fool ordered me not to leave my office until it was time to activate the weapon."

He picks me up, but I keep myself limp. He takes me over to his desk and places me on top of it.

My adrenaline spikes.

"I look at you now, and I see a little boy whose ambitions were far too unrealistic," he pauses for a moment, and I don't risk a peek. "I took pleasure in killing your parents."

His words cause my eyes to flash open in a fiery rage, and I grab the gun that he left lying by my head and aim it up at him.

He slaps it away, and I lunge off the desk and slam him into the wall.

"What a treat!" he says, his one eye burning with excitement. "I get to kill you myself!"

I slam my knee into his gut, and he swings a fist into my face. We send and receive strikes, but he gets the upper hand when he slams his forehead into the bridge of my nose, breaking it and sending a stream of blood to spray out of my nostrils.

I stumble back, and he slaps me across the face and throws me into his desk, sending paperwork all over the place. I charge, but he throws another punch, hitting me in my already broken nose.

I stumble back again, but this time I dodge and counter his punch by hurling my foot into his knee cap.

He buckles to the ground, and I drill my fist into his face as hard as I can, over and over again.

He pulls a knife and thrusts it my way, but I lunge, pulling my own blade out.

"You can't win, Jason," he taunts, languorously getting to his feet.

My eyes narrow, "Watch me, piss-face."

He grits his teeth like a maniac and charges at me. I sidestep before thrusting. I miss, but just barely.

We swing our knives at one another. We're both too fast to get hit.

I finally get a lucky swing and slice his cheek open, but he retaliates by stabbing me in the forearm.

I shove him into the wall and stab him in the hip.

He throws his elbow into my face, and then he thrusts his knife into my Kevlar vest.

I rip the knife out of his hand, pitching it across the room. I stab him again, this time in the shoulder.

He throws his knuckles into my left eye. I flinch back, giving him the chance to rush for the gun lying on the floor next to his desk.

I chase after him, but he reaches the pistol. We fly to the floor, and he pulls the trigger, sending a bullet through the ceiling.

"Go to hell!" I blurt, thrusting my knife into his side.

He aims the gun and pulls the trigger, "You first!"

My eyes widen as scorching pain hollows through my bicep.

He kicks me off of him, and I sprawl out on the floor, blood spurting from my wound. He jumps on top of me, pounding my face. Each strike forces more and more life out of me.

"Rebirth can't bring you back if your brain is destroyed!" he yells with an evil grin on his face. "So, let's make sure there's nothing left of your skull!"

He brings the gun up to my head, and four gunshots go off in the hallway outside. The quick distraction allows me to slap the gun out of his hands and break his nose with a punch to the face. He falls off of me and Raphael rushes in. His mask is off, and his face is twisted in rage.

I watch as he kicks Matthew in the face over and over again, "You! Spineless! Worm!"

Matthew grabs his foot mid kick and twists it, forcing him to the floor.

I get to my feet and rush over, grabbing my murderer by the collar and hoisting him upward. I throw him against the single window in the room, cracking it. I slam his face against it again and again. He reaches his hands back and grabs my face, digging his nails into my flesh.

I stumble back, screaming as my lust for revenge erupts. I reach up, grab his right wrist, yank it off my face, then snap it like a twig before kneeing the small of his back and forcing him forward into the window once more, shattering it and leaving stray shards sticking out in certain places.

"Kill him, Pinder!" Raphael blurts, getting to his feet. "Kill him now!"

Matthew sneers, "He can't kill me! No one can! I'll just keep coming back!"

A primal cry of rage bursts from my lips, and I slam his face down into one of the stray shards. The tip jabs through his good eye and sticks into his skull.

I reel his head back and slam it down, sending the shard further in. I repeat the hit, blood staining the window sill. Filled with rage, I slam his head down again.

Raphael spits on the floor, "He won't be coming back from that."

I don't respond, instead I push Matthew's lifeless body out the window. I stand with my hands trembling at my sides. My legs give out and force me to my knees.

That man shoved me headfirst into this hellish reality. He killed me and family, slit my best friend's throat, made me who I am.

Images of my mom, dad, and Simon spiral through my mind.

It's finished. You three can rest now.

Despite the stab wound in my forearm and the bullet hole in my bicep, I feel sheer electricity.

Raphael looks at me, "Every single Saint and Reaper in the area is either dead, or running for their lives. We won."

I look up at him, "How many of us are left?"

"Not enough."

"Where's Chloe? Is she alive?"

He nods.

I stand. Blood rushes out of my broken nose, "Let's shut the God Code down."

Dante enters the room with a remote in his hand, "The weapon has been locked up; there's no way to access it. But one of those scientists gave me a remote in exchange for his life."

I wipe some of the blood off of my face, "What are you waiting for, then? Shut it down."

"It isn't that simple. Mills prepared for something like this, that's why there's no kill switch on the remote. There is just a way to control the blast radius."

"Those two scientists installed a kill switch on the device, remember? We have to gain access to it."

"Kid, the wall that blocks it off can withstand a rocket launcher. There's no way in without a code, and only the elites have it."

I spit some blood, "What about another car bomb? Don't you think that would do the trick?"

Raphael shakes his head, "Too risky, it could detonate it."

I grit my teeth, "So all of this was for nothing?"

Dante tosses me the remote, "Like I said, we can control the blast radius, but the lowest setting would still wipe out all of Seattle. Mills told us Reapers how the device could only be set off once, so once we do this, it's all over."

His words bring me hope, "We could use that as an advantage."

Raphael raises an eyebrow, "Showing the population that Mills was trying to kill them?"

"Yeah. By setting it off, we can show everyone what Mills was planning. The God Code detonates, and they'll all turn against him."

Dante nods, "Agreed, he'll try to pin it on us, though."

"Not if we pin it on him first," I reply. My bicep is burning, my forearm is stinging, and my nose is throbbing. "We need to get back to Seattle, evacuate the people there, and show them all that we're the good guys."

Raphael smirks, "I like it."

Dante glances down at the remote, "We'll need to be quick. The virus will hit the city within an hour. It's slow spreading, but a single inhale, and you're dead."

I pick my mask up off the floor, "Let's get a move on then."

CHAPTER FORTY-FIVE

My radio crackles to life, and Dante's voice pours through, "Are we sure about this? The second I press this button, there's no going back."

I bring the walkie up to my lips, "We have no other choice. Mills still has the other remote, and we need to end this now . . . detonate it."

"Alright." A moment later he says, "There, it's done."

His words mute the silence. The waves seem to lose their voice. I slowly put my radio away.

"We lost practically everyone," Chloe says. Her voice permits the small waves to utter some whispers against the dock.

It's midnight, and the sky is cloudless. We can see millions of stars glimmer above.

The smell of salt and fish fill my nostrils.

"I know," I mutter, rubbing my bandaged up wounds. "But we don't have time to mourn, not just yet. Now that the weapon's been set off, the siren should be sounding at any second, and Raphael along with the others are going to hack into the system and broadcast a message to every single screen in America. We won."

"Not yet," she disagrees, her blonde hair moving around with the sea breeze. "We still don't know who the population is going to side with."

Someone steps up behind us, "And Mills is still breathing."

I turn around to respond to Kennedy, "Presumably."

Chloe raises an eyebrow, "Why aren't you with the others."

"I have the shakes, man," he replies. Dried blood is stained to his face. "I just wanna get out of here. We have just a little over a half hour until this entire place is overrun by the virus, and I don't want to go out like that. I don't think any of us do."

"We'll be fine," I say, getting to my feet. "We can easily outdrive it. It's the innocents I'm worried about."

Chloe sighs, "It was either this, or let Mills flood every state with the virus and all of us die."

Kennedy shutters, "Can we talk about something else?"

"Like what?" I ask.

"I don't know, just not that."

Chloe rolls her eyes, "Baby."

He glares, "Just because you don't have a soul doesn't mean that you get to bash me for caring about other people, alright?"

She gets to her feet, "No soul, huh?"

"That's what I said."

I shake my head, "Calm down, you two."

He turns to me, "You know I respect you, Jason, but I'm tired of her picking on me."

"Since when have I picked on you?" Chloe asks.

I sigh, and the emergency siren goes off. I knew it was coming, but the sound triggers something inside me, and my heart begins pounding. Memories of the day Simon died play through my head, and I stop the lump from forming in my throat.

He's dead, Simon. Matthew White is dead.

Chloe looks at me, concern sweeping across her face, "What's wrong?"

"Simon. I just miss him."

She embraces me, resting her cheek up against my pounding heart, "I know, me too."

Kennedy stands still, "Uh, who's Simon?"

She moves away from me and stares at him, "Obviously someone who was really important to us."

"Geez, I was just asking."

"You talk at the worst times."

"You know what, Frye? You're just—"

Gunshots a few blocks away stop Kennedy from finishing.

I stuff my hands into my pockets, glancing at him, "Go meet up with the others, alright?"

He looks as if he's about to argue, but second guesses himself, "Yes, sir."

He turns, walking away and flipping Chloe off.

She glares, "I'm gonna stomp on his balls when he falls asleep tonight."

I remove my left hand from my pocket and place my arm around her, pulling her in close, "Go for it."

Dante's voice replaces the ominous siren, "Attention citizens of Seattle, this is a city-wide evacuation notice; a poisonous gas is going to flood your homes and will kill you with a single inhale. Please gather your loved ones and get as far away from here as possible."

He goes quiet for a moment, then repeats the message.

The radio clipped to Chloe's belt suddenly goes off.

"Frye?" it's Raphael. "Frye, you copy?"

She unclips it before lifting it to her lips, "Yeah, what's up?"

"You and Pinder are at Colman dock, right?"

"Yeah, why?"

"There's an emergency. There's another dock off to your right – Pier 57 – it's where the massive Ferris wheel is."

"I'll be right there."

"Come alone."

"Come alone? Why?"

No response.

She and I exchange looks, sharing similar expressions.

"What was that all about?" I ask, ocean spray sprinkling my exposed neck.

She shrugs, "No idea, but he seemed desperate."

"You should get going, then."

"What're you going to go do?"

"Meet up with the others. When you're done with Raphael, come find us."

"Okay," she kisses me on the cheek before jogging away. I watch her blonde hair swaying back and forth.

My chest burns with emotion as I watch her leave. I can't help from smiling and allowing my shoulders to relax with the thought that our fighting could be coming to an end.

I leave the dock, glancing at the ginormous Ferris wheel off in the distance. I pick up my pace and run to the rendezvous point. Raphael should have finished his task of exposing Mills, so the remaining Lazarus members will be there.

White's death has released me from my greatest weakness. The lust for revenge is gone. I'm free, and now the only person that stands in the way of a better tomorrow is Mills.

Lazarus will put him down like a wild animal.

Next time, he won't be walking away, and it will certainly be more than just a slit throat.

I'm going to make sure he's incapable of resurrection.

Someone jogs out from an alley, and the two of us crash down to the ground. I ready myself for a fight, but my adrenaline diminishes when I see it's Raphael.

"Raph?" I ask, my fresh bandages turning red from the abrupt fall. "What are you doing here?"

"What do you mean? I was on my way to come find you and Frye."

"She's on her way to go meet you, remember? You radioed her in."

Even in the darkness of night, I can see the whites of his eyes get bigger, "What are you talking about?"

"I was there, man. You radioed her in, told her it was an emergency."

"Pinder, my radio broke during the fight at the facility."

My blood runs cold, "But it was you – I heard your voice."

He hastily gets to his feet before pulling me up, "Where did this person tell her to go?"

"Pier 57."

"Start running."

I nod, and the two of us sprint toward the pier. Dante's voice echoes throughout the city, telling everyone to evacuate before it's too late.

My lungs burn as my speed reaches its peak.

Who was on the radio?

People are flooding the streets. They are panicked and racing for their cars, but we ignore them, pushing past each scared individual, vaulting over the hoods of vehicles and screaming at everyone in the way to move.

We pass the Colman dock without slowing down.

We keep running until the radio clipped to my back pocket goes off. It was almost inaudible due to the evacuation notice.

I skid to a halt, unclipping it and bringing it up to my lips, "What was that?"

Kennedy's voice comes through, "You're leaving without us?"

"What are you talking about? We're on the streets."

"Cut the crap, I'm literally watching you right now! How could you? What type of leaders leave their own people behind? And of course you're bringing Frye!"

"Kennedy. . . where are you?"

"What does it matter. . .? You don't give a single shi—"

"Shut up and listen to me carefully," I order. My voice is filled with panic. "Raphael and I never left, we're still by the docks. Where are you? What do you mean you saw us leave?"

"I'm nearing the Ferris wheel, look behind—"

I stuff my radio back into my pocket and run with Raphael at my side. We finally arrive at Pier 57. It resembles a mini carnival, and it even has whimsical music playing from an overhead speaker.

"Kennedy!" I call out, my eyes darting everywhere.

No response.

I walk further down the pier, my heart pounding, my lungs filled with acid. It's dead quiet, and there's not a single sign of life anywhere. This place is abandoned. There's no sign of Chloe, or Kennedy, or *us*.

"I found something," Raphael says.

He kneels in front of a puddle of blood.

Approaching him, I say, "There has to be a security camera around here."

"Yeah, right there," he points to a camera hanging from one of the booths next to the blood.

"Now we just need to find where the security office is."

"No need," he stands, pulling a cellphone out of his back pocket.

"A phone? How is that going to help?"

"Not a phone, a device that can hack and watch footage from anything that records."

"And you just so happen to have one on you?"

"I never leave home without it, and good thing I don't. We needed an entry code for the building that held accesses to the system that controls the city's evacuation and P.A. system, and we would've never gotten it without it."

He taps a few buttons on the device, waits a moment, then flips it sideways.

I step to his side, and watch the footage of the two of us standing by the puddle of blood. He swipes to the right, and the footage rewinds. He scans the footage until he spots something that catches his eye.

We both watch. My jaw falls wide open and I begin to tremble.

I watch Chloe walk onto the pier and approach Raphael, who's wearing something completely different than what he's wearing now. The two of them talk, but there's no audio. A figure creeps up from behind and puts a black hood over her head, wrapping both arms around her neck and smothering her until she goes limp.

The man impersonating Raphael drags Chloe's unconscious body to a small boat, tossing her in it. Her body smacks against the floor.

The figure who smothered her is wearing a ski mask, but he takes it off and throws it into the boat. His face is never clearly seen.

That's when Kennedy shows up, hiding behind the booth we're currently next to. He pulls out his radio, but before he can speak into it, a figure shows up behind him and jabs him in the side of the throat with a combat knife.

Kennedy collapses to the ground. The figure bends over and finishes the job, and before my mind can fully comprehend what it's seeing, he turns toward the camera, flashing it a crude snarl.

It's me.

He flips the camera off before lifting Kennedy's body and dumping the corpse into the ocean. The imposter gets in the boat.

Raphael starts the motor, and they speed off. The rippling wake forces Kennedy's body to sway up and down violently.

"What the hell is going on?" I growl.

Raphael shakes his head, putting the device away, "You're asking the wrong person."

"They have Chloe, we need to get her back!"

"We can't, not now."

"Are you kidding me?" I grab him by his collar. "Two doppelgängers just kidnapped her, and you won't help me get her back?"

He grits his teeth, shoving me back, "Look to the horizon, culero."

I turn and look, seeing an endless cloud of yellowish mist approaching the docks. I see nothing beyond it, and it'll spread through Seattle in just a few minutes, killing us all.

People are still frenzied as they run through the streets. Children cry out for their parents, husbands leave their wives behind. Cars crash into each other.

Raphael grabs me by the shirt and drags me along with him. My thoughts are scrambled. I can't breathe.

The mist creeps forward.

Chloe.

ACKNOWLEDGMENTS

I want to start this acknowledgment off by thanking my superhero of an editor, Stacey. You've changed my life and have made my dreams come true. None of this would be possible without you, and I can never thank you enough. Your countless hours working on *Revolt*, and *Mutiny* have truly shown, and you're like a second mom to me.

I'd like to thank my loving parents for the support. Mom, you've spent so many hours on cover designs, logos, and so much more, and that has really made my novels come to life. I know I can be a bit of a brat sometimes, but I'm so thankful for you and I love you so much. Dad, thank you for always believing in me and promoting my book like an absolute boss—a big chunk of my first sales were because you pushed and pushed for everyone to check it out, and for that, I'm so grateful. I love you, homie.

Here are a few shout outs to the people that made Mutiny possible:

Natalie, my amazing girlfriend, thank you for motivating me on those days where I didn't even want to look at my keyboard. You've inspired me to work harder and write better each day, and for that, you're my favorite. Oh, by the way, "UwU."

Teagan, I've always said that you're the Simon to my Jason (not like you're dead or anything), and I wouldn't even be writing if it weren't for you. You're the bomb.com, and I can't wait to see you again.

Liz, I can only imagine your face while reading this! You've always had amazing feedback for my books, covers, and just about everything else. You're one of the few people that got to proof read *Mutiny*, and I cherish our friendship. Keep being you, my dude.

Tyson, you were literally the first person in my friend circle to finish *Revolt*, and that means so much to me. You rocked being Jason in my second trailer, and I'm honored to call you one of my best friends.

Matthew, even though you haven't even finished the first book, you've always been so supportive of my writing, and were one heck of a Reaper in my trailer. You've always been there for me and had my back. Thank you so much for everything.

Liv! Oh, dude, I don't even know where to start! You've spent so many hours helping me promote, film, and edit my trailers. Even though I'm a total butthead sometimes, I hope you know that I couldn't have done any of this without you.

Issiac, my man, I spelt your name wrong in my last acknowledgement despite being one of your best friends since I've moved here, so I'm correcting my mistake. Thanks for all your involvement with the trailer and promoting my book to everyone you know, even as far as creating a fan page.

Genevieve, you're my sister from another mister, and I thank you for that oh so delightful shake you bought me over four months ago. See, I haven't forgotten! I haven't! But for real, though, I've known you my whole life, and I'm so glad that we grew up together.

And lastly, thank you readers for picking up a bit of my soul and reading it. You guys are seriously amazing, and I hope you all know how appreciative I am to every single one of you. I love the fan art and all the feedback. Reach out. I love hearing from you! Also, reviews help me out so much. Every review is appreciated, please support indie-authors by reviewing their work. Again, thank you all.

ABOUT THE AUTHOR

Benjamin Vogt fell in love with writing at the age of 12. His first book in the *Revolt Trilogy* was his debut novel. Now, a seasoned 17-year-old author, he has published his second book. When not writing, the Idaho native can be found river rafting, camping, rubbing his cat's belly, enjoying a good nap, or sharing spicy memes with the boys.

facebook.com/kljshadfjh

instagram.com/author_benjamin_vogt

COMING SOON

BOOK 3 IN THE REVOLT TRILOGY

AMNESTY

This Winter